Michael Khatkar

TORTUREDLOVE

A novel of life, death and hope

Michael Khatkar

TORTUREDLOVE

A novel of life, death and hope

MEREO
Cirencester

Mereo Books

1A The Wool Market Dyer Street Cirencester Gloucestershire GL7 2PR
An imprint of Memoirs Publishing www.mereobooks.com

Tortured Love: 978-1-86151-406-6

First published in Great Britain in 2015
by Mereo Books, an imprint of Memoirs Publishing

Copyright ©2015

Michael Khatkar has asserted his right under the Copyright Designs and Patents
Act 1988 to be identified as the author of this work.

The address for Memoirs Publishing Group Limited can be found at
www.memoirspublishing.com

The Memoirs Publishing Group Ltd Reg. No. 7834348

The Memoirs Publishing Group supports both The Forest Stewardship Council® (FSC®) and
the PEFC® leading international forest-certification organisations. Our books carrying both the
FSC label and the PEFC® and are printed on FSC®-certified paper. FSC® is the only
forest-certification scheme supported by the leading environmental organisations including
Greenpeace. Our paper procurement policy can be found at
www.memoirspublishing.com/environment

Cover design: Ray Lipscombe

Typeset in 10.5/15pt Bembo
by Wiltshire Associates Publisher Services Ltd. Printed and bound in Great Britain by
Printondemand-Worldwide, Peterborough PE2 6XD

Prologue

When a child miraculously appears from the womb, the anatomy of the universe violently erupts. Every atom rearranges itself, and the essence of the Earth is distorted forever. The magical creation of two human beings is blessed with an almighty talent to metamorphose and reconstruct the world, and it will continue to do so even at the point of death. Every breath, every step, every word, every microscopic action, will buckle the blueprint of nature and design a new strategy and pattern. The world is continuity, a vast kaleidoscope of instability and undisciplined change, and every person is a catalyst in its ceaseless, reactive capability.

You are an integral piece of the timeless universe jigsaw, a boundless blank canvas which will create a unique picture - because you exist.

For all the people who have influenced and inspired the course of my life and for the handful who make it complete. Thank you!

Also by Michael Khatkar: 'Motivation From A Tortured Mind'

Contents

CHAPTER ONE

Hope

'I can see, I can see, I can see!' The piercing shriek of the voice of the patient in the bed next to Rebecca's was unbearable. For ten tiresome days it had resonated through the ward and woken the other patients, and Rebecca had been unable to sleep. The man had continued to mutter, scream and broadcast his discontent with the world and his putrid existence with vitriolic profanity night after night.

Rebecca and the ward's third patient had both requested a move away from this clearly tortured, demented soul, or asked that at the very least he should be moved to an isolated ward where he couldn't disturb anyone with his shameless insanity, but their pleas had fallen on deaf ears. Typically, the hospital was at bursting point. All the patients could hope for was a speedy recovery for the hollering maniac, so that they could all return to their normal lives.

Three nurses and a doctor rushed to see what the commotion was. The rest of the patients watched with disappointed, bleary eyes. There was little else to do in the middle of the night other than hope that this latest delirious nightmare was his last of the night. Unfortunately, this particular midnight drama had only just begun.

Rebecca's stitched forehead wound was pulsating angrily. Thanks to her intensifying resentment towards the imbecile, it was

1

now brewing an evil concoction of intolerable pain and glaring hatred. As warm blood trickled out of the gash, blurring her left eye, she called over to the gaggle of nurses for assistance.

None of the medics tending to the screaming madman acknowledged her appeal for help. They were all standing around his bed rapturously clapping their hands and whooping for joy. Something had clearly happened tonight, for they were all, including the patient, ecstatic. Rebecca and the other patients could only hope that this dramatic scene heralded the departure of the psychopath.

Finally one of the nurses noticed Rebecca's blood-soaked dressing and the forlorn look of sheer agony and desperation on her swollen face. She tended to the bleeding wound and apologised for the noise coming from the now curtained bed next to hers. 'The poor bleeder's been blind for months and he's suddenly got his sight back' she explained. 'It's a miracle, we never expected him to see again.'

The nurse was clearly moved by the mumbling psycho and was barely controlling her tears of elation. Rebecca didn't really comprehend the vastness of the 'miracle' in bed fourteen. It was now dawn, she was extremely tired and her own mental anguish, along with her gaping wound, was crushing any sympathy for the crackpot who had been driving her crazy for ten very long and tiresome days.

The nurse injected her with a soothing sedative. It was a most welcome escape from the unwelcome din as it rushed through Rebecca's veins. At last she drifted off to the safe haven of her dreams.

His hand was large enough to exert a vice-like grip on the back of her head, like a five-tentacled octopus entwined around her cranium. He mercilessly pushed her forehead into the window with an almighty muscular force emanating deep from his tensed abdomen. With his other hand stabilising his body against the wall and helping to direct his brute force, the torture was bloody and relentless. The sickening smash of her skull, eye sockets and nose against the strengthened glass splattered blood over the pane, smashing her once-pretty face and splashing red over the glass.

His fingernails seemed to sharpen and lengthen as they penetrated the curved bone of her head and pierced into the soft matter of her brain. Crunch, crunch, crunch, each forced encounter against the window became softer and softer as more of her skull crumbled and deteriorated, exposing the oozing grey matter it had been designed to protect. With one last almighty assault, he leapt half a metre into the air and with a simultaneous war cry of 'Die, you bitch!' he thrust her face into the window. Her head collapsed. His hand felt the sharpness of broken glass and the cutting edge of the criss-crossed steel wire that ran through it to give it security and strength. There was now nothing distinguishable left of her face. The tip of her vertebral column jutted out from her neck as her lifeless body slumped back into his heaving torso, leaving blood, crushed eyeballs, bone and twisted, grey mush from her brain spewed everywhere, akin to a manic, abstract piece of art that had been rabidly created by an agitated and frenetic artist.

With a loud, frenzied scream, Rebecca abruptly woke and sat up in her bed. Her incessant and brutal nightmare had struck again.

The other patients, accustomed to outbursts of human noise, didn't even flinch at Rebecca's brusque awakening. The ward psycho was slowly trundling past her bed after what seemed like a trip to the window. No wonder he had such a frozen, dejected look on his face; the view was anything but inspiring.

The psycho slumped down onto his bed and looked tearful and crestfallen. Rebecca was still agitated by her vicious nightmare and now she felt had that familiar seeping warm sensation from her forehead. Ten days had now passed and her wounded head hadn't healed. It continued to discharge copious amounts of blood every day.

'Are you OK?' she reluctantly asked the psycho.

He looked up. His eyes were watering, wide open and cloudy with redness.

'No, I'm not OK. I was expecting a different view from the window. I just don't understand.'

Rebecca was intrigued. 'What the hell were you expecting, what don't you understand?'

'I was told, day after day, that the grass is damp and dewy green, littered with thousands of gorgeous reddish-brown autumn leaves that delicately waft to the ground from the huge oak tree right outside that window. I was told that right next to the tree is a sprightly, flowing brook. I was told about how the sparkling water cascaded and trickled over the pebbles and glistened in the winter sun. Where is it all? There's nothing out there, nothing at all.'

He was clearly mentally disturbed, as his disappointed hostility poured out. He continued through a fury of tears, inanely ranting about the missing view. 'Where is it? Where's the oak? Where's the grass? Where's the sunshine?' With every word he was getting louder and angrier.

One of the other patients who had been listening chipped in. 'Who the bloody hell told you that? Who told you that was the bloody view?'

'It was my angel. It was my nurse. Every day she told me about the view, every day she told me deep, deep inside my heart I had to believe I would see again. She told me that even if I had only one tiny ounce of hope left that one day my sight would return that I had to hang on to that, because that one ounce of hope would get me through, that single ounce would give me a reason to live. She always told me that all I needed was hope. Just hope, and nothing else.'

The fourth patient in the corner, who had been quiet until now, decided it was time to conclude the deluded conversation.

'Can't you all see he's not very well? Please leave him alone. As for you Michael, I'll break the sad news to you darling. You haven't had a visitor in weeks and weeks. I was here before these two arrived. Every day you mumbled to yourself about the view and about having hope. It was all you, no one else. Hope was a shining light for you. It was probably that very hope that encouraged your eyes to see again, because the nurse had told me you were unlikely ever to have your sight back. So whatever happened, be grateful that your vision has returned. Maybe the angel was all in your own heart and mind.'

There was silence in the ward. Michael began to sob himself to sleep in the belief that a bizarre twinkle of hope had literally saved his life. Rebecca called for the nurse, as her dressing was once again drenched with seeping blood and the pain had become insufferable.

A few hours passed. The familiar clink and clatter of cheap mugs filled with weak hospital tea stacked on a trolley, pushed by an annoyingly cheerful catering nurse, woke Rebecca from yet another violent dream. Michael was sitting up in his bed, bizarrely looking quite normal, compared to the deranged look he normally had. His eyes were still painfully swollen and Rebecca remembered through the clouded memories of the night before that he had miraculously regained his sight.

There was a nurse at his side, holding his hand, apparently explaining the unusual string of events. His transformation was bordering on ludicrous, from the cantankerous, bitter foul-mouthed pig he had been no more than twelve hours before to the pleasantries and smiles of a gentleman.

The ward matron delicately removed Rebecca's dressing. The wound was still bleeding profusely. The pain was unrelenting, and even after ten days of suffering it still sent an agonising jolt of distress into Rebecca's concussed mind. This was the most destructive affliction a human being could experience. The physical damage was mixed with her mental anguish and her horrendous memories.

She sat up and repeated the same routine she had become accustomed to over the last few days, cautiously dabbing her forehead, whilst the bleeding stitches were left uncovered for an hour or two.

The four-inch diagonal laceration, swollen and pulled together with no less than twenty stitches, seemed an exposure of Rebecca's life, deep, wounding and harsh. The actual injury was no more than a peripheral rupture and barely represented a smidgen of the angst and torture that weighed so brazenly upon her existence. Lying in bed and waiting for the physical trauma to heal inadvertently exacerbated her mental trauma.

Time has the magical ability to heal all physical and emotional distress, but it also has the uncanny power of allowing perpetual and deeper thinking, causing further upheaval of the mental drains that one normally doesn't have the time or patience to lift and investigate. Those are the deep and calamitous sewers that nonchalantly flow in all our minds, borne of troublesome experiences and long-forgotten negative, often seriously hurtful, thoughts.

Rebecca's mental sewers were overflowing with heartbreak and untold misery. The drains had been well and truly lifted. Time had been a curse over the last ten days and hope had become distant and abandoned. Her tears expressed her deep-seated anxiety over a world that had brought her nothing more than violence, degradation and now the icing on the cake, an intense gash in her face, pouring with bitter, discontented blood.

If any time was perfect for discharging her secluded soul it was this moment of utter depression and melancholic regret, as blood trickled into her eyes and mixed with her sour tears.

It was sparked by a voice from bed fourteen.

'Deep, deep inside your heart you have to believe you will be OK again' said Michael. 'Even if you only have one tiny ounce of hope left that one day your face will heal, then you need to hang onto that, because that one ounce of hope will get you through, that single ounce will give you a reason to live. Sometimes all you need is hope.'

The man who had been the ward psycho walked over to Rebecca and repeated the sentence.

'I don't have any hope left' she replied. 'I don't even care about my face. My life isn't worth living, all I want to do is die. My partner did this to me. He laughed as he pushed my face into a pane of glass. See this criss-cross pattern on my forehead? It was done by the steel wire that was in the glass. He kept pressing my face into it until the wire cut through my skin.'

CHAPTER TWO

Vision

The window was an ephemeral opening into another world. It was Rebecca's escape from a hateful existence, certainly not one she had dreamt of when she and Jack had got married. For her, 'till death us do part' was the rock-solid vow for hope, vision and possibility, of living the life dreams are made of. All her life she had believed in the magic of romance, staring into each other's eyes and then gazing out at the world together with a beautiful, shared vision of the future. That had been nine months before, when their shiny wedding rings had bound them together for a wonderful, exhilarating life ahead. Now the same rings, severely tarnished, had become manacles of disdain and solitude. Rebecca would often sit in the window, tearful and exhausted, blankly glaring into the unaware world and wondering where it had all gone so dreadfully wrong.

After only two months of marriage they had had an argument, surely the everyday kind that thousands of couples around the world are having at every single moment. In the provocative haze of cross words and raised voices, Rebecca couldn't recall how a petty argument had somehow ended in a back-handed smack straight across her face, the force of which had knocked her to the floor and left a hefty bruise where Jack's hand had ruptured the blood cells underneath her soft porcelain skin. That assault should have been the warning sign, the neon-flashing beacon signalling danger, evacuate, leave and never look back.

Jack was shocked and apologetic. He didn't know what had overcome him, where the rage had emanated from or what had triggered the uncivilized and heartless slap. His apologies extended to an expensive restaurant dinner, chocolates and Rebecca's favourite flowers.

The bruise had disappeared after a few days, but a horrific new chapter in Rebecca's tortured life had begun. During the following seven months Jack had metamorphosed into a possessive, overpowering, explosive monster. Their god-fearing wedding vows had become a curse that laughed and jeered at Rebecca, who had so easily and foolishly fallen under their spell of misguided romance and transcendental possibility.

Every bruise on Rebecca's slight, once-beautiful body told a stinging tale of terror and pain. The blemishes ranged from run-of-the-mill pinches where loose skin on her lean body had been grasped between Jack's thumb and finger and mercilessly twisted until blood vessels burst, to sexual aggression, which pitifully had become the only way Jack could achieve arousal.

'Don't laugh at me, you bitch, don't laugh at me!' he had warned. But Rebecca wasn't laughing at Jack's inability to get an erection.

'I'm not laughing at you Jack, I never laugh at you, don't worry, these things happen, we can sort it out' she pleaded.

'You bitch, you're laughing at me, it's all your fault you've made this happen. If you were sexy it wouldn't happen, you're a dirty bitch, it's all your fault, I can sort it out you bitch, I don't need you to sort it out, I will!'

At which point Jack had pushed Rebecca's head into the pillow until she was gasping for air. With a punch to her face, he became aroused and capable of penetrating her trembling body. For her it was a black eye, which she explained away at work as a clumsy incident; for him it was the beginning of insane sexual power, a route from which there was no return. Violence was now the impotence-beating aphrodisiac, the one thing that injected him with masculinity.

Rebecca deteriorated rapidly, from a confident, effervescent star who lit up any room she floated into to a reclusive, soft-spoken, cowering introvert, incapable of flicking even a light switch without dwelling on the ramifications. Once a personality that brightened rooms, she was now a quivering wreck who was too frightened to turn on a light bulb. Rebecca now lived in a dark, destructive world, a tunnel with no light at the end of it, a long endless corridor of blackness, pain and dread. Her entire being had been eclipsed by a remorseless bully, whose unsuccessful life and sexual infirmity were exclusively blamed on Rebecca and yet powered and negated by inflicting her with appalling injuries and indelible mental scars.

Jack's life was enormously successful now, with a soaring career and a colossal appetite for sex. Seven months of torturing, belittling and desecrating his wife had transformed him from an irrelevant nonentity to a towering skyscraper of a man, overflowing with arrogance, power and confidence. Behind every successful man there is a woman. In Jack's case his woman empowered him, filling him with tremendous gusto to succeed. Rebecca meanwhile had been plunged into a life of rape, distress and tribulation, a life that made the idea of death appear like a beautiful summer breeze in a meadow of bright flowers.

Jack's new-found depravity escalated his income, in direct proportion to the unjust mental and physical perversions which he casually bestowed upon Rebecca. It was just as well he had cajoled and browbeaten her to leave work and become a housebound servant. The bruises, the ruptured lips, the limping and the meaningless, haggard expression in her eyes were all getting too difficult to explain to her colleagues.

Her last day at work had been wrecked. She had never actually arrived for her own departure. On that particular day, Jack's insecurity alarm had sounded, as it often did, at the prospect of Rebecca's colleagues taking her out for an affectionate farewell lunch, so he had left her handcuffed to their bed. She had lain there for ten long hours, delirious, helpless and wounded by the frantic rape of the night before.

Ironically, she was relieved when Jack returned from work. It meant freedom from her imprisonment and most of all the stinging rancid, stench of her own urine that she had squirmed in all day. Jack fed and watered her and once again that night subjected her to horrific cruelty, partly punishment for soiling the bed while she was tied to it and partly to recharge his prowess after a demanding day at work.

As Rebecca cautiously sat on the window ledge a searing jolt of pain electrified her body. Even sitting down had now become a chore. It was a grim reminder of three nights before, when, following another testing day at the office, Jack had needed to liberate his angst in the only way he knew how by imprisoning the frail, battered Rebecca for a night of indiscriminate, inhumane misery. His assault had begun with slow tender kisses over Rebecca's war-torn landscape of a body and rapidly escalated into uncontrollable miniature bites that were bizarrely more pleasant than the usual brand of aggression he devoted to her.

This sexual placidity was a deceptive stepping stone to the debauchery that was to follow. A counterproductive and disagreeable day at work had left Jack feeling weak, unsuccessful and vulnerable, and he desperately needed the blood raging back through his veins in preparation for another heady day in the office tomorrow. Rebecca's unexpected, momentary lapse into shivers of biting ecstasy immediately crumbled as she experienced a new level of supreme agony. This was demonic, the epitome of shameless violence. Her tears overflowed as she simultaneously screamed and clenched the pillow with her teeth. The pain cascaded through every morsel of her convulsing body. Jack, in his exuberance to reclaim his rightful masculine security, had taken a square inch of Rebecca's plump, soft bottom into his eager mouth and in a second of barbaric degradation, vigorously gripped it with his teeth, clamping his jaw like a ferocious rabid dog and with all his might, pierced her skin and torn a mouthful of bleeding flesh and muscle from her writhing body. There was a warm, bloody chunk of human tissue in his mouth, awkwardly stimulating the taste buds on his tongue with stringy dense gristle between his teeth. Jack had descended lower than ever before in his malevolence towards his wife, and Rebecca had ascended to a previously-unknown level of suffering. He was elated, strong and virile. She was paralysed with pain and reduced to an emotionally numb carcass of raw meat, better off dead than alive.

Rebecca's world was now detached from reality. As she peered through the steel wire-laced security window, she remembered the sales pitch from the eager estate agent who had persuaded her and Jack to buy the property. 'It's got some interesting, quirky features, but there's a lot of space. Once upon a time it was an asylum. In the days when they didn't know what to do with the slightly unusual people, they banged them up in here, that's why there's steel wire in all the windows. But look on the bright side, it's also a great security feature. Look at the view, it's amazing, it really is to die for. This place will make you both happy and I can just feel it in my bones, you'll just love being here.'

Rebecca was literally dying for the view. Every day she continued to exist (because this wasn't living) at the ironically named 'Happy Villas', she died a little more. She was lost, isolated and living in a torturous hell, unfit even for vermin.

As she looked through the criss-crossed wiring, her grand plan started to materialise once again and with a wry, slightly caustic smile she realised that escape from the vile bastard who had almost killed her physically and destroyed her emotionally was imminent, because he hadn't, even with all his depraved and grotesque wickedness, managed to kill her spirit. That smidgen of hopeful sparkle that hadn't yet been cannibalised from her body was the only ounce of hope she had, the only reason she hadn't yet committed suicide. Deliberately extinguishing her pointless life with an overdose or slashing her own wrists with a razor blade appeared immeasurably more congenial than another night of Jack's ungodly contamination and debased mentality. And yet, somewhere deep in the hidden depths of her damaged, worthless, shattered heart was a microscopic adventure. Every day Rebecca spent in Jack's cancerous clutches chipped another scrap from her spirit, yet one day that light would illuminate a path of emancipation and Rebecca would live the life that had rightfully been granted to her the day she was born, a life that was temporarily immobile in this wretched underworld. Rebecca's contrary shred of vitality was the difference between life and death.

The accursed 'Happy Villas' was Rebecca's tortured love asylum, but her plan to run and never look back at the insanity she had inherited from this malignant sanctuary kept her dreams alive.

As her eyes fluttered shut, her head pressed against the cold glass, the sting from countless wounds that had motivated and inspired Jack to corporate and sexual boldness, temporarily subsided and the pacifying beauty of Rebecca's dreams soothed her star-crossed life, transporting her far from the doomed abyss she was incarcerated in into a world that was beyond harm.

The steely cold structure, with its unique angles and audacious engineering, stood as a beacon of opulence, indulgence and artistry. Towering above all its structural grandeur, it personified love, romance and blissful courtship. Sheer intrigue, passion and poetry, the Eiffel Tower epitomised the bliss and euphoria that Rebecca hungered for. Sitting at a round, white, ornate iron table, perched outside a café on a side street that branched from Champ de Mars, Rebecca was in awe of the Eiffel Tower soaring into the sky with an astute sublime eminence. Her mind was hazy with romantic anticipation as she waited for her beloved admirer to arrive and delicately kiss her rosy, blushing cheek, then focus his eyes into her soul. Then without a single word he would make passionate love to her. This was the embodiment of fairy-tale, lovesick preconception. It bordered on the delusional, yet it symbolised the monumental significance and interpretation of love itself.

Rebecca closed her eyes and felt the warmth of the mid-morning Paris sunshine on her face. She could sense her suitor approaching and there was passionate *amour* in the air, washing over her, quivering through her heart and causing her skin to tingle. She shivered as if she was experiencing an icy blast of cold air, and the delicate hairs on her arms stood to attention. The premonition of her lover was stirring her sensuality into moist physical dampness, and every physical and emotional response to sexuality was avalanching through her frame. The fuse had been ignited and was burning with an enticing thrill. The anticipated kiss on her cheek would undoubtedly be the detonation, discharging a torrent of desire, bursting into the sky to share that exclusive, privileged space with the Eiffel Tower itself.

This was the love Rebecca craved and dreamt of, this was the love she knew was her god-given right to possess. This was the cherished dream that had coloured her fantasies and churned her romantic aspirations from childhood. This was the happy-ever-after that had infatuated her existence and kept the spark of hope alive.

A gift from heaven, carved by God himself, swathed in masculinity, the absent piece of Rebecca's chivalrous, romantic puzzle that completed her life had arrived. Standing in front of the Eiffel tower, Rebecca quivered with flaming delight as the key unlocked her heart and blood scrambled through her veins, precipitating a feverous, sexually-enchanted euphoria.

'Hello my love, I've been waiting for you all my life,' said the handsome stranger.

'Who the fuck have you been waiting for all your fucking life?'

Rebecca's spellbound ecstasy imploded. The earth cracked as the white ornate iron table, the café, the Champ de Mars and the Eiffel Tower, along with the romantic magnetism of Paris and the warmth of the mid-morning sunshine, plummeted headfirst towards the fire and brimstone of purgatory.

Jack had arrived home earlier than usual after a disciplinary hearing at work, one that had been brought against him through a complaint of sexual harassment from a female colleague. Rebecca had been sleeping after another sleepless night during which Jack had used her already broken body to prepare himself for his hearing. She hadn't stirred as Jack had entered the room, not even whilst he had intently watched her smiling and muttering to her dreamy Paris lover.

Rebecca's shock awakening as her dream returned to her hellish reality, in that momentary second of confusion caused her to blurt a mixture of dazed words that further fuelled Jack's instability, remorseless anger and reckless jealousy.

'I was in Paris, I was with... I was with no-one... it was you,

Jack. I was talking to you. Yes, it was you. Who else could it be? We were in Paris and I love you, I love you Jack. I've waited for you all my life.'

Rebecca sobbed frantically as she tried to explain her beautiful Paris dream, but she knew there was no way through this hideous dead end. Her already injured heart and tortured mind were preparing her wrecked body for an onslaught of bloodshed as her dream turned into a living nightmare. Even the horrific experiences Rebecca had already witnessed through her tumultuous, vulgar marriage couldn't adequately prepare her for the tyrannical violence that awaited her.

Jack had been reprimanded and severely humiliated that day at work. The serious case of sexual harassment against him, heralded by his ever-increasing obnoxious confidence, was likely to be the end of his career. The mounting evidence against him, including numerous witnesses who were all too willing to testify against this hard-hearted bully, was immense. To discover his wife dreaming about a lover pushed any modicum of decorum, sensibility and common sense away. He was now on a free-fall mission of revenge and destruction. He had only one route of deliverance - Rebecca.

Insecurity, jealousy, fury and a grave incapacity to think before acting is a hazardous concoction, one that has resulted in butchery on a grand scale, worldwide devastation and genocide. It has wrecked entire chunks of history and changed the face of civilisation. Today, Rebecca was about to face the reality of his mindless fury.

There was a sickening crunch of bone as Jack grabbed the back of Rebecca's head like a grapefruit within his palm and crushed her nose into the window, flattening her face, whilst he shouted 'Can you see Paris now? Look, look! Look at Paris, look at your lover, he's running away, ha ha, he's gone!' Rebecca threw up, gushing an acidic brown bile from the depths of her empty stomach and spewing it onto the cold glass, clearing the mist that had been created by her petrified breath.

'Look at you now, look at this mess, no one wants you now, you disgusting bitch. He's run away! He's gone, you bitch, he hates you! Go and chase him, go on then, Go! Go! Go! Go! Go! Go!'

With each shout of the word 'Go!' Jack pressed Rebecca's injured face harder into the glass. The force on her facial bones was immense and blood poured from her cracked nose as the strengthened glass began to splinter under the pressure.

Rebecca delicately wafted away from the miserable damnation, her soul incapable of any more pain. She left her body with an enchanted smile on her face and transcended to the only genuine comfort humans are blessed with, the comforting elixir of a mother's embrace. Mum stroked her beaten forehead and straightened her bedraggled hair. All was peaceful again as the god-given tranquillity of a mother's arms dulled the pain of tortured love and a mutilated life.

'What are you smiling at, bitch? What's so funny? Let's see if you find this funny!'

The glass threw in the towel and cracked in defeat as Jack pulled back Rebecca's head and pitilessly smashed it into the window. Razor-sharp shards of glass penetrated her skull. The steel wiring remained strong, making a last stand and searing a chequered imprint through Rebecca's skin until it reached the hard bone of her skull.

After nine turbulent months of marriage, Rebecca was mentally demolished and physically maimed, broken of spirit and broken-hearted. Her childhood dreams were a shattered window, a jaded view, a discoloured vision. Hopes had been dashed, spirit had been extinguished, vows had been broken and an innocent life had been destroyed beyond recognition.

CHAPTER THREE

Possibility

For two whole days Rebecca had remained unconscious in bed thirteen, until the blind ramblings of the simpleton in bed fourteen had finally awoken her. This was a life she didn't want to wake up to. She cursed God for not having taken her final breath, for not allowing her the peace she had earned in heaven for the pain she had suffered on this evil earth. What else could she possibly endure?

Michael was missing an angel. He had conjured hope deep within his being and that raw, subconscious optimism had whispered life back into his eyes and through his despairing darkness had once again showered him with light. Now he was committed to immortalising his divine epiphany into a path of mental recovery for Rebecca. He had materialised as her angel. Having discovered that a whisper of aspiration kept his heart alive, he was now encouraging hope, vision and possibility into another darkened, dead soul who was bereft of any hope of surviving this beastly ordeal called life.

Every day, he held her frail hand and whispered the same assurance to her: 'Deep, deep inside your heart you have to believe you will be OK again. Even if you only have one tiny ounce of hope left that one day your face will heal, then you need to hang onto that because that one ounce of hope will get you through, that single ounce will give you a reason to live. Sometimes all you need is hope.'

Outside bed number thirteen, Rebecca's life was the epitome of hell, not just the basic satanic underworld but the lowest level of hell imaginable, even lower than the eternal level Judas had been imprisoned in for his biblical atrocities. Her husband had already been bailed for his crimes and he awaited her arrival with clenched, bloodstained fists. Her family were absent. They had ostracised her because of him and her home was ironically an asylum, an asylum that had once housed the criminally insane and now had bequeathed her an insane existence. The four walls of the hospital ward had become her utopia, Michael her angel, and hope her only weapon against the atrocious, villainous world that was eagerly awaiting her return. That was Rebecca's expectation. Death would be a release from a life of pain and regret. However there was a distant glimmer, a shining star, light years from reality but nevertheless still a shining beacon of hope. Breathtaking possibilities had been syringed into her veins, alongside the pain-numbing sedatives, through Michael's attention. There was a faint possibility that a beautiful, endearing life was possible. Maybe, just maybe, the pathway to the land of milk and honey was littered with degradation. Rebecca had already stepped every vile, humiliating inch of that path and was severely bruised and battered. She was cautiously and unwillingly preparing herself for a sunrise that was ready to shine its light onto her, a sunrise that could light a doorway into a world of enchantment and the life she was born to live. After all, before every glorious sunrise there is darkness, a darkness you have to experience before you truly see the light.

'Live your life and set the world on fire. Come what may, keep your ray of hope alive, keep it deep within your heart, etch it into your life and don't ever forget, every fire started with an insignificant, microscopic spark. Hope will guide you and hope will keep you alive.' With those words from Michael ringing in Rebecca's ears she left the safety and comfort of the hospital that had nursed her back to health and qualified her for the cruel world again. But this time she had a renewed strength, a vigour pulsating through her veins, a power that had been absent since her dreams had been shattered. Her head was swathed in bandages which were gradually healing her physical lacerations, which still sent jolts of juddering pain through her brain and limbs, but her mental restoration had begun. Every pinch, bite, punch and violation of her mind, body and soul was glued together with hope and inspiration into a sturdy foundation from which she could evolve into the person she dreamt of being.

Now every solid restored brick of belief and hope that had been stacked into a fortress of stability and substance around Rebecca's heart fragmented into dust. Her clenched fist of fortitude turned to a handful of sand, seeping away until her fingers were empty. All it had taken was an angry, growled sentence from Jack as she stepped into his waiting car.

'About fucking time, do you know what you've fucking put me through? Three weeks of hell, while you lay in bed making the most of a little cut that you asked for. I've nearly lost my job and I've lost weight, just because you had a little fucking cut. I should have finished you off when I had the chance. You miserable bitch, you can take that fucking bandage off too, you look even stupider than usual.'

Rebecca had already begun to blame herself for the ordeal that was awaiting her, regret was repeatedly bellowing the same perennial question 'Why didn't you tell the police the truth?' 'Why didn't you tell the police the truth?' Why didn't you tell the police the truth?' The investigating officer couldn't take the enquiry any further, Rebecca had corroborated Jack's flimsy story that it had been a freak accident. It was a blatant and transparent lie, everybody could see that but they were powerless to take any action. No matter how much the police officer attempted to coax the truth out of Rebecca, she perpetuated the absurd charade that Jack was innocent. Rebecca had clearly committed the greatest crime in helping Jack evade the law and escape the pricey debt he owed to humanity, for the crimes against his own spouse.

The ten-minute drive back to the asylum was a soul-destroying trip back to reality as Rebecca's mind attempted to filter the vile insults spouting from Jack's mouth, with Michael's antidotal words of hope but as Rebecca carried her own luggage back into the familiar penitentiary known as home and saw the boarded window she'd had her skull pummelled into, tears poured from her eyes. Her heart was shattered, and along with it all hope of regaining a normal life was destroyed. Every minuscule ounce of possibility was crushed and her vision was once again metaphorically blind.

'What the fuck are you crying for, you selfish bitch? I suppose you wanted to go to Paris. I'm the one that should be crying because you came back. Now fucking get over here and learn how to be a good wife again before I make you kiss another window.'

Jack grabbed Rebecca by her frail arm, the medical wristband still intact on her wrist, a reminder that she had left the warm sanctuary of hospital less thirty minutes ago. He pulled her into the kitchen.

'Come here bitch, you need this more than I do,' he snarled. Rebecca knew what was coming. She blanked her mind as Jack pushed her head into an empty pizza box on the kitchen worktop and forcefully kept it there with the same hateful familiarity he had pushed her head into the window. Her face was crushed into a piece of left-over pizza as the pungency of mouldy cheese and tomatoes wafted up her nose. Blood filtered through the layers of her bandage. The pain from her forehead told her that the wound had reopened. It was an unbearable, sickening, distressed pain and yet it was a meagre inconvenience compared to the anticipation of the odious and callous rape which was about to happen.

Jack forcefully pulled down Rebecca's trousers and abruptly fumbled with his zipper, pushing her bleeding face harder into the pizza box. She floated into another dimension somewhere between the ambiguous haze of reality and fantasy. He crunched her nose further into the left-over food and forced his enraged manhood into her broken, quivering body. He began shouting inhumane blasphemies and insults at her, periodically slapping her naked bottom and leaving her skin stinging red.

Rebecca was watching this detestable drama unfold from above. She had surpassed human capability and was witnessing her own bloodthirsty debasement in action. Yet the very essence of her life and spirit were slipping into oblivion. Rebecca was dying.

This was not the life she had been born for. What had happened to the hope, vision and possibility every born child is blessed with? Why was her life so cruelly evaporating into a meaningless void, dissolving away at the detestable hands of an evil tyrant? She was placed into her mother's arms to have a rightful, happy part in the world, to live a life of purpose, belonging and aspiration, one that contained minimal pain and maximum probability of prosperity and satisfaction. Every opportunity to live a consecrated existence had been welcomed with open arms. Every day, every week, every month, every year was a dignified collaboration with the universe, its people and its environment. A miracle was now being wiped away, harshly sodomised into the skeletal hands of the grim reaper. Death was waiting to guide her passage into the afterlife. The cessation of her life in this harrowing, dishonourable manner was just a few breaths away.

Rebecca's mortality stairway had opened, and there was a blinding light magnetically drawing her towards it, brilliant white, calming and blissful. Jack's verbal abuse was dampened and echoing in the distance. She could feel no more pain as she started to glide towards the divine presence of the celestial stairway and to her creator. She looked down at the hopeless, spiritless lump being pounded to death, expressionless and damned. The time had come to wave goodbye.

Suddenly a thought thunderbolted through Rebecca's mind. Even the angelic, beckoning light lost its hypnotising power, as a string of words appeared as an alluring beacon in every cell of her body and numbed her into stillness.

Deep, deep inside your heart you have to believe you will be OK again. Even if you only have one tiny ounce of hope left that one day your face will heal, then you need to hang onto that because that one ounce of hope will get you through, that single ounce will give you a reason to live. Sometimes all you need is hope.

The stairway closed, the dazzling light disappeared and Rebecca crashed back into her body. She opened her eyes as if a bolt of electricity had shot through her. The pain of the torture returned with a vengeance, along with a sudden urge to fight this despicable oppression.

Much to Jack's surprise she pushed back as he pushed himself into her. In that split second of intensified pain she managed to open the kitchen drawer and slip in her hand, grabbing the first object she could feel – a wooden handle. It was a kitchen knife. With all her might she pushed her head up from the pizza box and kitchen worktop and threw back Jack's hulking frame. In an impassioned moment of sheer anger and desperation, she turned around to face her bullying, rapist husband. Then, with all her vitality, with every ounce of strength she could muster, she drove the knife into Jack's gut, until her clenched fist stopped it from going any deeper.

His face contorted as Rebecca forcefully turned the knife in his stomach until warm blood was gushing over her knuckles and spurting over her body. With a final attempt to grab her he collapsed over her, and both of them dropped to the floor in a pool of scarlet blood. Rebecca had freed herself from their binding vows 'Till death us do part' and called the Police to inform them of her victory.

Death had become the only answer. Jack had been exiled from his rightful place on earth and would now be accountable in purgatory. His crimes against Rebecca were irrefutable and his underworld punishment appropriate.

As Rebecca was marched away from the bloody crime scene, she caught a glimpse of her window, shattered by her head. Through the splintered remains she saw a serrated image, tall, overpowering and victorious; the Eiffel Tower. Rebecca smiled.

Hope had fortified her broken heart and inoculated her soul, dragging it back from the bottomless pit her life was decaying into. From the point of no return she had retaliated, resolutely fighting her way back to the life promised to her when she was born. That insignificant spark of hope was all she needed. A singular ounce of animated promise had kept her alive.

CHAPTER FOUR

The Child Psychologist

Millions of minute transmissions through millions of microscopic cells, an imagination that knows no boundaries, has no limits and can conjure magical, inspiring thoughts and soul-destroying visions within the blink of an eye – Rosie had studied the complexities of the human mind for her entire career as a child psychologist.

Overcoming her traumatic, penniless childhood, where hard graft had been more important than a formal education, Rosie had fought epic battles against an embittered, downtrodden, socially inept family to win the success she desired. Every day she would play the projector in her brain, detailing with precise accuracy and inspirational colour the way she wanted her life to be. Everything was elaborated in Rosie's internal film, from escaping the constraints of her debilitating family circle and its jaundiced thinking to her university education and the career that followed, one that would alleviate the mental anguish and struggle that many people witness throughout their childhood. Years of positivity had paid Rosie prosperous dividends. Every detail that played in her mind had manifested into reality.

Personal mental development had rocketed Rosie through her life, propelling her through anguish, challenges and obstacles that would have defeated most people. At the age of thirty Rosie was exactly where she had imagined at twelve that she would be then. Every morsel of her being had been created through her own mind. She had accurately determined the life of her dreams. Opportunities were strewn in her path, not through some magical mysticism but through having a positively developed outlook which subconsciously opened her eyes to things that others with less developed minds would have missed. That was the capability of her potent mentality, viewing life through the eyes of optimism and imagination.

For the first time during her eight-year career, one in which she had helped many troubled and tormented children, Rosie could not assume the consummate posture that had carried her through life. Sniggering, malicious doubts that had been previously banished to the innocuous section of her brain came marching out of exile and were now squeezing their corrosive, discriminating poison into her governing thoughts. Her entire attitude was suddenly, venomously negative as this malignant reasoning attacked the cerebral virility and psychological strength she had relentlessly built over almost two decades.

Seventy-two hours earlier, Rosie had received the customary mandate assigning yet another problematic child to her expert care.

Referral from Chance Secondary School – Wednesday 17th July, 2pm.
This child possesses a delusional imagination, bordering on psychotic hallucinations, culminating in horrific nightmares - needs immediate attention and regulatory assessment. Possible danger to himself and others.

It wasn't a particularly outlandish assignment. On the contrary, it was bordering on psychological normality for prepubescent teenagers to have angst-fuelled, torturous thoughts, causing untold anguish to themselves and their families.

Wednesday 17th July was just another day in Rosie's accomplished life. However at 2 pm a meeting with an irksome teenager was about to spark a strenuous chapter in her roller-coaster life, in which she had maintained a promising high point for over a decade. One otherwise insignificant encounter that would leave her unadulterated world teetering on the brink of freefall collapse, the rollercoaster was about to plummet, with gut-wrenching unpredictability.

After a generous, home-prepared lunch washed down with copious amounts of rich, dark coffee, Rosie was ready for her afternoon session. She stepped into her office full of her customary anticipation and steadfast optimism. This was another opportunity to encourage a young turbulent life onto the path of steady mental rejuvenation. In the majority of cases that were sent to her, tempestuous urchins just needed someone to listen to them and understand their agitated uncertainties, typical of those created by many disjointed family structures. Rosie's own disordered childhood and burdensome family instilled useful experience into understanding the rough and toilsome instability of growing up and the riddles it provoked in an imbalanced juvenile mind.

A prevailing aroma of old oak and worn leather embraced Rosie as she opened the door to her office. It was a smell that always evoked a sense of success, as it was in this very office where Rosie's career aspirations had culminated. Unknown to her, this brief encounter was about to reshape her fulfilled life.

Three walls of Rosie's office were adorned by towering oak bookshelves, on each shelf a library of human psychology and personal development, two subjects that were permanently etched into Rosie's heart and pertinent in the evolution of her thinking and consequently her entire life.

The young lad with his raven black hair hadn't noticed Rosie sweep into the office; his gaze, much to Rosie's delight, was transfixed by the bookshelf opposite him as he scrutinised titles such as 'Without hope the heart truly dies', 'Think and Grow Rich', 'Overcoming Mental Abuse', 'The Power of Positive Thinking' - four titles that had been instrumental in Rosie's personal success.

'Are you interested in these books?' she asked him.

The boy turned to acknowledge Rosie's question. His deep, pitch-black eyes were wide open as his poignant glare met her face. His expression was a disturbing mix of distress and irritation.

'No I'm not, I wasn't looking at the books. There are evil eyes staring at me from the bookshelf.'

The combination of those unexpected, unnerving words and the fretful look on the boy's face sent a convulsion of panic and discomfort through Rosie's body, as if she had been dipped into a bath of stinging ice cubes. She felt a distinct sense of shock. She too had witnessed 'evil eyes' staring out from the bookshelf. For eight years she had inspired delusional, perturbed individuals to normality, whilst witnessing the full spectrum of conditions from fallacious illnesses to clinical depression, but this boy was different. His expression and his words were obviously sincere. Either he really could see evil eyes staring, or he was the greatest living con artist. For Rosie, it was the former. Within minutes of being in his company, the evil eyes were haunting her again.

In her agitation, Rosie stumbled around her desk so she was facing the boy. Swiftly turning to the bookshelf, she pulled out the four books and abruptly slammed them onto the oak desk in front of him, sending surface dust scurrying into the air in the dimly lit room.

'Are they still staring? She said nervously.

The boy pointed at the gap from where the four books were removed and with a shrill in his voice screamed, 'Yes, they are!'

The intensity of his stare was driving into Rosie's brain, but she managed to compose herself and force calmness into her voice. She chastised her inner self for being fooled by this obvious childish prank. *Stop being so pathetic, stop being so pathetic, stop being so pathetic,* she repeatedly told herself, furious at being outsmarted by a teenager. She decided to beat her patient at his own game by asking him some searching questions, then watch him flinch and stutter as his lying was unearthed.

'Ok, describe them to me.'

Without a second of hesitation or any of the tell-tale signs demonstrated by liars, the troubled boy blurted out, 'They are blood red and angry, they want me dead. They want to kill you too, they are looking at you. They're burning into your head. You're going to die. You're going to hell!'

Rosie was dumbfounded and breathless. Her composure had been ripped to shreds by a clearly bewitched, malevolent boy. She shouted for his parents who were waiting outside and literally marched them all out of her office, uttering some nonsense about having to leave immediately.

17th July was without question the worst day of Rosie's adult life to date. She had faithfully followed her heart in every aspect of her career and today she had crashed and fallen to her knees. How could she have been deceived so majestically and fallen in such an unsophisticated manner? How had an insignificant, twisted little monster duped her into questioning her own sanity, a mental state that she had fortified for so many years?

When she arrived home, feeling shrivelled and crestfallen, her unsuspecting husband Rick bore the brunt of her anger and anxiety. After two hours of feverish conversation and calming wine, the angst had been converted to raucous laughter and contempt for the world in general. Rosie had returned from her personal hell and had gleefully convinced herself that some vicious little runt had made a clown of her. She went peacefully to bed.

Rosie didn't have to turn around to know that the heavy, freezing cold hand on her shoulder wasn't friendly. She was filled with dread and nervous panic, fearing the worst. Blood-curdling images paraded through her mind, raising her temperature and sending tremors through her body. She felt scared and vulnerable. Her natural reaction was to run away and fight an overpowering temptation to look back and see who the hand belonged to.

She imagined that her legs were quivering as she gathered speed, precariously navigating her way through the dark, foggy mist that was clouding her vision, but her attempts to escape her assailant were futile. It wasn't his hand that she could feel now but a cold steely breath that seemed to be repeatedly on her neck. He was so close, but he couldn't quite grab her. She was just one minuscule step ahead of him. She could feel a scraping pain intermittently running down her back, as if he was reaching out and attacking her with something sharp. It seemed he was penetrating her skin, because she could feel a trickle of blood. 'Rick, Rick, Rick, where are you?' she cried, but her husband was nowhere to be seen.

The lacerations were getting deeper, the pain more intense. Rosie knew there was blood running down her legs, and the cuts were bleeding heavily. The breath on her neck was getting colder. Why was he chasing her? Why was he attacking her? Who was he?

Rosie's willpower and strength wilted. She fell to her knees, her body convulsing in fear. She could sense the dark doom that was now inevitably hers. Her fate was sealed in dripping blood and a repulsive, unprovoked crime was about to happen.

From her trembling kneeling position, with tears of terror running down her cheeks, she turned her head to face her attacker.

A threatening black-cloaked figure stood in front of her, head tilted downwards, with a hood hiding his face, leaving it in darkness except for his grinning, remorseless, blood-red eyes, satanically burning into her crying face. This was Death.

Rosie knew she was damned and that her mournful, pathetic protestations were meaningless. The cloaked figure raised the curved silver blade and slashed it across Rosie's neck, separating her head from her body. Simultaneously, she woke up.

Rick woke to see his wife sitting upright in bed, gripping her neck with both hands and screaming at the top of her voice. He finally managed to calm her down, but sleep would not return.

Amid Rick's relentless snoring, Rose stared into the darkness, wondering how the last twelve hours had turned her into a quivering wreck and how her usual mental agility and tenacity had been stretched to breaking point. There wasn't an answer to her conundrum. Thought-provoked insomnia had now set in and she couldn't shake the horrific images of her nightmare. In the end she decided that trying to sleep was a losing battle, and a hot, soothing drink was the best solution.

Two cups of tea later, Rosie's tired mind had calmed down considerably. Her diabolical nightmare had been confined to the depths of her sleepy mind, and it was time to rest before dawn presented the challenges of a new day.

Sleep came easily now and she drifted into a deep, blissful rest, hoping to sleep through till morning. However the two cups of soothing tea she had drunk had other plans, and soon persuaded a lethargic plod to the toilet.

The carpeted bathroom floor seemed colder than usual, like dewy grass after a frosty night, and Rosie could see her own cold breath billowing into the air. There was no fooling Rosie's astute senses a second time. This was clearly another episode inside her own troubled mind. However, this time she was alert and determined to face and defeat her demons. After almost a decade of working with young tortured souls, she had learned some valuable lessons in personal mind manipulation, including the ingenious talent of repressing habitual nightmares and converting them into favourable outcomes.

The bathroom light flickered, and the temperature seemed to plummet further. The dewy grass now felt like cold, hard concrete, and the mirror had frosted over in a frozen, misty glaze. Rosie's mind was awash with images of her childhood battles, when no challenge had ever been powerful enough to ambush her into submission. Her veins flowed with hatred as she recalled the cause of her nightmares, her ghastly 2 pm patient.

As the nightmare returned death was on his way to complete his eternal mission, the mission to cease life. Rosie had mere seconds before he was going to decapitate her again, but this time she was ready. This time she was going to conquer her fear and exterminate the plague of death and insecurity forever. She was determined.

She pounded around the bathroom searching for an appropriate weapon to attack the evil-cloaked entity who she knew would reappear any moment. Nothing was going to shake her morale, not even the gruesome appearance of the word 'DEATH' in the frosted bathroom mirror.

The door handle turned; he had arrived. Luckily Rosie, having come from a large family and a one-bathroom house had locked the door; even in her dreams she was cautious. She pulled out drawers and swept over the glass shelves with her hands, frantically searching in vain for a useful implement, as the banging and pushing on the bathroom door became more violent. At last, the only weapon Rosie could find - an electric toothbrush. At least it had a strong, sturdy shaft which she could dig into his intimidating, evil eyes. She fully understood the necessity to outwit the mental plague. Physically attacking her nightmare ghouls, even with a toothbrush, was all that was required. Rosie knew that the sentiment behind the action was enough to stave off and control her visions.

She let out a blood-curdling war cry and gripped the toothbrush, then thrust it above her head. 'C'mon you bastard!' she growled. Then she unlocked the door.

The immense surge of confidence within Rosie's dream state gave her the upper hand. After all, she knew it was all her own imaginative fabrication. Her strategy worked just as she had anticipated. She had regained control of the indomitable darkness, and all his power of the underworld, governed by Satan himself, almost quailed into insignificance as he saw the expression on Rosie's face and heard her furious scream.

She had scared death. She knew that if she could maintain her courageous stance, her tortured mind would be liberated. This was the time for unrelenting superiority. Death was monumental, but Rosie had to scare him into insignificance.

With remorseless anger Rosie plunged the toothbrush into the bloodless murk of the hood, aiming for his repulsive, sepulchral eyes. She felt the soft, nauseating squelch as the toothbrush entered his flesh and he crashed majestically at her feet. She had thwarted her trepidation and overwhelmed the loathsome eyes of hatred and horror. Rosie had won her life back.

A ray of blinding brightness and certainty shone over Rosie's face as she stretched and woke. She was elated and optimistic that the world was back in her favour and her fears had been ceremoniously quashed. She turned her body to give Rick her customary morning greeting by putting her arm around him, a daily declaration of her gratitude to the world and indebtedness to a wonderful and supportive partner.

He wasn't there.

It was not her bed.

One hundred trillion individual, life-pumping, ergonomic cells blitz the human body with a diagnostic complexion of their own. Beyond microscopic, they create and prolong the vital force that keeps us alive. They all felt a shudder, a volcanic eruption, as she realised this wasn't even her bedroom. Rosie's mind collapsed, her soul crushed into confused oblivion. The only reaction she could muster was involuntary. Scream after shrill scream was followed by an unceremonious gushing of filthy, acrid bile from the disarranged pit of her stomach. It seemed an eternity before three people she didn't recognise, dressed in white, entered the dull magnolia-coloured room.

'Who are you, who are you? Where is Rick? I want my Rick!'

Without a single word, with barely an acknowledgement of the bizarre, unintelligible scenario, two of the figures held Rosie sternly by the shoulders and with considerable force pressed her down into the bed, the vomit still dribbling from her mouth as she spat the disgusting vileness at them, intermingling it with her deranged, confused screams. The third person powerfully gripped her jittery, weak arm and coldly pierced the pale skin with a needle, syringing into her body the contents of a phial. The three people firmly held the agitated, trembling Rosie until she drifted into deep sleep. Then they cleaned her face and replaced the crisp, white cotton sheets with fresh ones. They left the room with the same sneering disdain with which they had entered it.

The sun shone through the window, the familiar morning rays of warming light shining their bright optimism and stirring Rosie out of unconsciousness. She abruptly woke, to find a hand wrapped around hers.

Delight and comfort washed over her as she recognised the familiar voice. It was Rick. Tears of relief and joy welled up in her eyes.

'Hello sweetheart, how are you feeling?'

Rosie looked up at him. It really was Rick, the love of her life, but words couldn't formulate in her mouth. She could hear them in her mind perfectly, but couldn't transfer them into sounds to greet him with. Every word turned to an incomprehensible child-like sound as she tried to express the thousands of bewildering thoughts rampaging through her mind.

The overwhelming question was - why was he wearing a large black eye-patch?

CHAPTER FIVE

The Asylum

It was Wednesday 17th July, and Rick was not expecting the emotional discharge that was being fire-bombed at him. Rosie had been mentally bludgeoned by a fourteen-year-old boy. Rick was far less temperamental than Rosie and could only think of one course of action, simply to beat the living daylights out of the obnoxious little bastard who had left his dear wife teetering on the brink of a nervous breakdown. Naturally, being far more headstrong and irritable than his wife, he was unable to step back and see the reality through the choleric mist that was blinding his judgement.

Rosie was in a state of abstract disturbance, whilst Rick was prepared to murder a fourteen-year-old. Neither of them, in their subjective, illusory frames of mind, could focus on the actual validity of what had happened. The miscreant patient, albeit wickedly unprincipled, was not the protagonist in this melodrama, but he was, understandably, the catalyst that lit the fuse.

In the end they went to bed, simply concluding that it was just one of those days and that the world was full of despicable brats like the one she had encountered earlier in the day.

All night Rosie was restless and unsettled in her sleep, and at one point she took ten minutes to compose herself, following a detestable nightmare in which her head was sliced off in a horrific attack by the grim reaper himself. Rick did his utmost to calm her nerves and quickly drifted back to sleep.

Rick was a heavy sleeper, but his senses after such a turbulent and eccentric evening were on high alert, particularly when he heard clanking, banging and crashing noises coming from the bathroom. This was tedious and annoying. Without a second thought he leaped out of bed, noting that Rosie wasn't lying next to him, so she was presumably responsible for the sounds coming from the bathroom.

He tried the handle, but the door was locked.

'Rosie, Rosie, Rosie, open the door!' he shouted.

'C'mon you bastard!' came the reply. The door opened, and he just had time to take in the savage look in her eyes before she plunged an electric toothbrush deep into his right eye socket, crushing the soft, gelatinous eyeball and penetrating the frontal lobe of his brain. He collapsed, yet somehow through the pain he was still able to restrain his possessed wife and dial the emergency services.

Rosie had suffered delusional psychosis and total mental disambiguation. She was not deemed responsible for the unprovoked attack on her husband. She was in a state of unpredictable acute insanity and was admitted to the only organisation that could cope with such an illness, the inappropriately named Happy Villas Asylum.

There was no actual treatment at the asylum; it was merely a place where they observed and sedated patients day after day until they showed signs of recovery. For three weeks Rosie was kept restrained. For three weeks her unconscious existence plagued her with atrocious illusions of death, the grim reaper and images of the evil red eyes which had originally incited her mental decline. Every day Rick had visited her and watched her staring into a void, talking to entities that only she could see, and every day his heart crumbled a little more. Would the love of his life, the one who had left a black hole where his eye had been, ever come back to the real world? Would she ever return and repair the equally black hole in his heart?

None of the reports detailing Rosie's demise into mental breakdown made any sense, and as each day passed Rick's contempt for the world and the caustic young patient who had sparked this monumental reaction within his beloved wife flourished uncontrollably, with fantasies of calculated revenge. Contemplation of the agonising torture he wanted to bestow upon the twisted patient prodigy that had caused such harm was the only nourishment keeping Rick's deteriorating mind alive and energetic. Even on Rosie's birthday, as Rick sat with her in the magnolia confinement of Happy Villas Asylum, slicing her birthday cake, he imagined that the soft, jammy buttercream sponge was the childlike flesh of his fourteen-year-old enemy, obscenely smiling at the pain his slow death would be rightfully causing him.

Today Rick's temperament was once again borderline psychotic, pushed further into the fanatical abyss so that Rosie barely recognised him as he walked in with her surprise birthday cake. The asylum wardens had relaxed the overbearing security measures and happily joined in with Rosie's celebrations. The voices as they all sang 'Happy Birthday' were clanging and bellowing in Rosie's ears, echoing through her mind and shivering through her brain. Three people joyfully singing was enough to disturb her irrational fragility, and she caterwauled and screamed as if she was fending off an obscene physical attack. 'Leave me alone!' she screamed as she thrashed around her bed.

Rick and the two wardens hurriedly grabbed the remains of

her party food and left the room. Rick helplessly watched on the security monitor outside the room as Rosie continued her bawling rant. These outbursts were common, and Rick would often view the heartbreaking drama as Rosie punched the air, fighting her invisible enemy, her eyes enraged with satanic fear. It was never safe to be in the room with her, as her indiscriminate lashings would frequently be aimed at those sitting beside her. Watching her demonic ramblings was soul destroying, and this was a world that Rick would never have envisaged becoming embroiled in. What had become of his beautiful, calm, intelligent spouse and the harmonious life he had once known?

As Rick pondered the many questions rambling through his despairing mind, there were two poignant things that the security camera was unable to scan, two invisible aspects that were about to disrespectfully twist life into yet another abnormal entanglement. First was the invincible presence, the cause of Rosie's angst and hysterical behaviour, the overbearing angel of death, cloaked in lifeless twilight with the damnable, raging eyes of doom piercing deep into her consciousness, always there and assuredly beckoning imminent death and destruction. Rosie understood that the reaper of darkness was beckoning her to the afterlife. She could no longer fight her destiny. The only way to beat the beast of hell was to join him in the abysmal shade, to finally wave farewell to the godliness of her earthly existence. It was time to depart.

The second thing that was concealed was one of the knives used to carve the party food that had been part of Rosie's birthday jubilations, a knife that Rosie had purloined in the hullabaloo of her tantrum.

'I give in, I give in, take me home, I want to go home, I want to go home!' Rosie's voice echoed from the speakers down the isolated corridor, Rick was powerless and lost. He desperately wanted his Rosie back. Unknown to him, he was about to lose her forever.

'Rick, I love you, I love you, I love you, I love you…' Rosie stared directly at the camera, as if she knew Rick was watching, and then, with tears pouring down her face, to Rick's horror, she brought her hand into view from under the crisp white duvet. She was gripping the orange handle of one of the knives used earlier.

Rick furiously banged the door to get Rosie's attention, but it was too late. With both hands now clamped around the knife, she plunged it deep into her chest. The knife seared through her hospital clothes, slashed her soft skin and sliced through her ribcage, plunging into her heart. She fell forward, and the whiteness of her bedding was drowned in a sea of deep red. Her warm blood surged from the wound.

Rick's frenzied banging and shouting for the wardens was futile; there was no saving Rosie from her hellish destination. The laceration in her heart was too severe. Despite the desperate attempts by the asylum staff and Rick to revive her and save her from the nether world, she wafted away and began her eternal journey into the bottomless pit of no return.

Such was the mournful demise of Rosie. Rick's life degenerated into freefall collapse. Living every moment without purpose or composure, he dedicated his reclusive, meagre existence to his decrepit bedroom, repeatedly staring out of the window and fantasising about the day when he would finally meet the scourge of his life, the wrathful individual who had murdered his wife, the fourteen-year-old boy who epitomised evil and had impassively ripped his heart out and left him to die. Every day Rick created a new dramatic adventure, and in each escapade the storyline was disturbingly familiar. The final chapter was always an appalling, torturous death for the child. The bloodthirsty closing lines of every story were the only thoughts that brought any form of solace to his crestfallen, emaciated days.

For almost a decade after Rosie's death, it was those graphic animations of the youth's slow, painful death that energised the vengeful blood flowing through Rick's distraught mind. He couldn't escape the vivid imagery of Rosie's suicide and the look in her eyes as she had sealed her fate with the knife he had carelessly forgotten to remove. Every single day another aberrant thought would corrode Rick's thinking with its anchor of regret and guilt, steadfastly mooring him to the past. There was no escape. He could not move on.

Happy Villas became central to the investigation of Rosie's suicide and it closed due to poor standards and accusations of misappropriation. The media concentrated on Rosie having access to a knife and the pitiful care and lackadaisical consideration of mentally-ill patients. For many years the grey dilapidated building remained boarded up, local folklore suggesting it was haunted by the melancholic ghost of Rosie, searching in vain for her beloved husband. The story of her death chilled people to the bone as rumours of devilish possession were spread by the hateful asylum wardens who had lost their jobs when Happy Villas closed.

Finally, a group of canny, prospecting bankers purchased the derelict property and converted it into modern housing. The sales pitch was polished and precise and targeted at young couples and newlyweds who were lacking funds but desperately wanting the first steps onto the prestigious property ladder.

'It's got some interesting quirky features, but there's a lot of space,' said the estate agent. 'Once upon a time it was an asylum. In the days they didn't know what to do with the slightly unusual people, they banged them up in here, that's why there's steel wire in all the windows, but look on the bright side, it's also a great security feature. The view is to die for. This place will make you both happy and I can just feel it in my bones, you'll just love being here.'

The young man and woman looked at each other. They hadn't even taken in the brief history lesson about the building they were viewing; it didn't matter. Their adoring eyes spoke volumes and shouted 'sold to the happy couple'. They had a romantic vision of a satisfied and content future. Seeing their smiles, the agent knew they were ready for 'Happy Villas'.

'Well Rebecca and Jack I can just tell when a property is perfect for someone, your smiles say it all,' she said. 'We can exchange contracts within a month, which if I recall will be just before you tie the knot. Congratulations! I'm so envious of the happy future I just know you'll have.'

CHAPTER SIX

Revenge

Tears welled and flowed under Rick's eye-patch. They would congregate into a puddle and then escape, spilling in one almighty tear. Today's melancholic waterfall was prompted by the news that Happy Villas had been sold to a young couple. At these moments of desperation Rick would trundle into his spare bedroom and stare at the undecorated wall; it was the only escape he knew, the only medicine that calmed his anger, loss and mental desolation.

Almost ten years before, following Rosie's death, Rick had converted the second room of his inadequate dwelling into a shrine for his dead wife. The entirety of one wall was covered with newspaper clippings and pinned notes, a labyrinth of connected information.

'Woman takes her own life at Happy Villas'
'Happy Villas set for inquiry into death of local woman'
'Director of Happy Villas in court over suicide'
'Happy Villas and the haunting suicide'
'Director of Happy Villas sued for negligence'
'Local man wins payout from his dead wife's suicide, Happy Villas to blame'
'Happy Villas condemned for closure'
'Happy Villas to be converted into homes'

Rick scanned the cuttings and placed among them the latest piece of news causing him untold anguish, within his vexatious world: 'Happy Villas – sold to the happy couple'. This supposedly uplifting piece of news, carefully cut from the local paper, had the opposite effect on Rick. It drove yet another knife into his broken heart. He turned his head to the other half of the mausoleum wall. This was the only antidote he knew, the only medicine he could trust to wipe away a decade of tears and merciless pain. The hairs on his neck excitedly stood to attention, and a shiver of anticipation rustled up and down his spine.

Directly in the centre of the wall was a note, the actual note which had originally been attached to it:

Referral from Chance Secondary School – Wednesday 17<u>th</u> July, 2pm.
This child possesses a delusional imagination, bordering on psychotic hallucinations, culminating in horrific nightmares - needs immediate attention and regulatory assessment. Possible danger to himself and others.

Upon Rosie's death, Rick had volunteered to clear her office. Among her professional belongings he had discovered the appointment notification that had sparked Rosie's surreal journey to destruction, the notification that had aggravated Rick's hunger for reprisal.

The concept of human revenge is a phantom of the mind, an irreversible pestilence that punishes its victim night and day, only ever relinquishing its compulsion when it is finally satisfied. It is a daily coercion fuelled by the clumsiness of vulnerable human emotions awaiting the powerful subsistence of retribution. For most people it lives and breathes with merely a fantasy acknowledgement that it will be fulfilled and an eye will be taken for an eye. The very thought of potential actions keeps it fed and buoyant. For Rick it was far more than a daydream; it had turned into a daily obsession, an addiction that had no other objective than complete consummation.

Surrounding the fateful appointment notification were reams of photographs and hand-drawn lines connecting and detailing movements, locations and the chronological life of the fourteen-year-old killer, who was now in his early twenties. The sizeable compensatory payout awarded to Rick, thanks to the negligence of Happy Villas, saved him from having to work, which was just as well considering his mental deterioration meant he was unemployable and far too unstable to take on sustained work. Instead he had committed his existence to the ultimate demise of his baleful nemesis.

The details mounted on the wall were laboriously intricate. It covered everything from details of his homes, friends and associates to the university the boy studied at, including his subjects and grades. For almost ten years the boy had had a one-eyed stalker watching and monitoring his every move. Rick was enslaved to his obsession with always needing to know where he was and what he was doing. His detailed knowledge of the boy's life gave Rick a surreptitious control over him. He knew everything about him, and that gave him the power to ultimately crush his enemy at any given moment.

There were two very different lives emblazoning the wall in Rick's spare room. On the left hand side, the tragic short life and death of his beloved wife Rosie, while on the right was every known detail of a life that would compensate for the loss of the life on the left. The latest newspaper cutting about the happy couple buying Happy Villas was the final nail in Rick's coffin, it was time to execute his revenge.

Rick's intuition sang out loud. Every ounce of his blood was compelling him to make the phone call. Today was the day his ten-year crusade for justice and vengeance was going to come to fruition. The little bastard who had taken his wife from him was only hours away from his long-overdue comeuppance.

Rick picked up the phone. This would signal closure and an end to the daily campaign that had relentlessly dominated every sleeping, waking, breathing day of his forlorn life, from the moment Rosie had plunged the knife into her heart.

'It's tomorrow, 9 am exactly, where I've told you. Half the money will be wired directly into your bank account tonight, the other half when you've done the job. Don't stop until you've taken his last breath,' he said into the phone.

That night Rick didn't sleep at all. He couldn't rest, eat or find any form of composure. Years of planning, hate and scorn were about to be consummated. Rick was incandescent with excitement and intoxicated by the contemplation of freedom.

It was a cold, frosty morning. Rick was standing around on a corner that he had adorned on hundreds of mornings before, cold and frosty, sunny and rainy. He had seen this corner through all four seasons of the year. The cigarette stubs from his visit only forty-eight hours before were still on the pavement. This was the precise position from which Rick had observed his adversary for eighteen long months, since his latest career move. Rick had attempted to thwart his plans in vain, with his usual onslaught of damning anonymous letters to the new employers containing a barrage of abuse, accusing the youth's boss of employing an evil-minded, twisted, degenerate murderer.

The timing was perfect. As punctually as a clock the boy appeared at the other end of the street, and the customary wave of homicidal thoughts steamrollered through Rick's mind. This was the figure of hate that plagued every second of Rick's pathetic life, and now Rick was about to witness his downfall.

As Rick lit his third nervous cigarette, three burly men with shaved heads, dressed in track suits and emblazoned football shirts, marched past him. There was a sense of brusque urgency in their heavy, regimented footsteps. Rick whispered to himself *Let the show begin, have no mercy, have no mercy, have no mercy, have no mercy!*

As the men approached the youth, Rick saw the look of fear in his face and quietly thanked God for the pleasure of seeing his dread. The men almost collectively nudged him aside, knocking him off the pavement onto the quiet road. Within seconds, before any words could be exchanged, one of them struck him directly in the pit of his stomach with a clenched fist the size of a small melon. The youth immediately recoiled in pain and shock, and Rick punched the air in gratitude. From that moment on the men were pitiless in their attack. The little bastard was completely defenceless as punch after berserk punch was rained upon his body. *Are you watching, Rosie? Are you watching my darling? This is all for you, this is for you, we've got him, I told you I would get him, I told you I'd get him back.*

Rick cried with happiness for the next three minutes as the beating continued. The men did Rick proud. They didn't stop until his blood had soaked his smart suit, his white shirt and the tie that had been so resplendent until a few minutes before. Then, without another word, they fled, and Rick left the crime scene, as jubilant and triumphant as if he was returning from the trenches having defeated the enemy. As he waltzed back home, he heard the sirens, the sweetest music that had ever graced his ears, knowing it was an ambulance speeding to scrape up what was left of his enemy. He grinned to himself and thanked God again for the wonderful opportunity.

The ambulance arrived to find the victim apparently seconds from death. 'What's your name, tell us your name?' said one of the paramedics as they scurried around the bleeding mess, pinpointing the wounds, inserting syringes and heaving him onto the stretcher. 'What's your name son? We're trying to help you.'

The man opened his and blurted out, 'Michael, my name is Michael, I can't see anything, where am I? Where am I? My eyes, what's happened to my eyes?'

As the ambulance careered towards the hospital, Michael slipped into a coma. Once again the world had regained an extraordinary balance. Rosie was never going to return, but the act of settling the score had given Rick a reason to smile again. His psyche was restored, and the images of Rosie's despairing suicide were fading. He wasn't normally sadistic or evil, but the memory of the young man being mutilated to death, having his life demolished right before his eyes, had put Rick in dreamland. The young man, his mischievous endeavours of scaring adults with his over-active imagination long forgotten, now lay precariously balanced between life and death. The high jinks of a carefree fourteen-year-old had levelled catastrophe onto the world. Three lives had now been wrecked.

CHAPTER SEVEN

Liberation

'Red Alert! Red Alert! Red Alert! Red Alert!' The twisted rope was grinding into the flesh of Rick's neck and the warning alarm had been activated. His brain was in panic mode. The vital oxygen supply had been restricted and millions of electronic synapses were exploding as they tried to attract attention. Brain cells were rapidly dying, and now Rick's body weight crushed his windpipe and snapped his neck with the ease of stepping on a dry twig. His brain could no longer communicate with the rest of his body as it dangled helplessly from the sturdy rafters. No oxygen-bearing blood was circulating past the constricting ligature as the pull of gravity tightened its lethal grip. Rick's brain was officially dead and minutes away from decomposing. There was no awareness or pain. One by one his vital organs began to shut down as the news of the murdered brain reached them. That heart, born to pump blood throughout Rick's body and keep his organs serviced, was instilled with one singular obligation, the simple understanding that at the end of its life it would be the last brave soldier standing. That moment of reckoning had arrived. There was no way forward, not without oxygen. One final salute to its fellow dead organs and the scarlet pump took its final breath. The pendulous body went limp as the rancid contents of Rick's bladder and bowels were simultaneously evacuated. The grand finale was a mammoth rush of air expelled from his lungs, like a huge sigh of relief, as his life was ultimately liberated. Rick was dead.

There was a silence in the room, interrupted only by the creak of the beam to which the carcass was fastened and the sound of bodily fluids dripping onto a newspaper beneath him.

The headline on the soiled newspaper had been the last straw.

BRUTAL ATTACK MAN LIVES

Following an unprovoked attack on a local man which left him struggling for life, doctors at Cove Hospital say his injuries are no longer critical and his recovery has begun. For a week it looked unlikely that the man would survive the assault, but he has now started to make a slow recovery. Police are searching for three suspects with shaved heads seen running from the crime scene. There is still no apparent motive for the brutal, life-threatening attack, in which the man was repeatedly punched and kicked with considerable force. Doctors say he is lucky to be alive.

The absolute indignity was unbearable. Rick's ten-year quest for retribution and redress for his dead wife had failed miserably. There was nothing left in his arsenal of revenge, nor was there an ounce of willpower to continue with an ordinary life. Defeated, lonely and hopeless, the only door left open for Rick was emancipation from this repugnant and meaningless existence. It was the only door that would reunite him with his Rosie.

CHAPTER EIGHT

Dreams

Prison serves a valuable purpose. The physical confinement of people and the deprivation of their personal freedom is an equitable right. Somewhere along the way someone made an error of judgement or showed deliberate resistance to the laws of the land, and for that they are confined. Whether for punishment or rehabilitation, prison allows their moral debt to be paid and keeps them isolated from the society they have chosen to dishonour and contaminate.

Prison inmates have desecrated the constitutional mandates bestowed upon the residents of a law-abiding commonwealth. They have broken the orthodox protocol that safeguards the right of people to live and be protected from harm. The prisoner has been incarcerated in a cold, dark, damp, cockroach-infested cell, with a limitation of basic privileges that are normally the prerogative of the masses. However that isn't the full extent of their imprisonment. The captivity that tortures them and yet inspires their rejuvenation and compensates for their crimes is located between their ears, within their criminal brains, thoughts and mentality. That is the greatest tribulation of all.

Rebecca had endowed herself with the most extravagant power

accessible to humankind, the sacrilegious judgement to undo the miraculous performance of god himself. She had ended a life, before the expiry date that God grants upon the birth of each person. For the freedom she had granted herself, the price was solitary prison entombment. As the knife had slashed into the guts of her evil husband, a remorseless burden had been lifted. Prison was an amazing reward, compared to the infringement of her right to live with her despotic spouse in the psychotic hell he had conjured for her. Her last recollection was the combination of warm, gurgling blood waterfalling out of Jack's stomach, the look of sheer surprise and horror on his contorted face and the beautiful serenity that wafted over her as his soul was delivered to the underworld where it belonged. This was one of the many movies that played in her mind. From the tortured love Jack administered freely to Rebecca's tortured mind, her brain was awash with the crooked path her life had taken and how her self-inflicted emancipation had resulted in her legal enslavement.

Rebecca's entire circle of friends and most of her family, except for one of her brothers, had ostracised her, banishing her for the heinous murder of Jack. The intensity of the media interest surrounding the case and in particular the details of the actual stabbing was too much for many to bear. Only Rebecca knew of the hell she was forced to march into, for the heavenly cause only she was forced to pursue. For her it was liberation from an iniquitous life; for them it was an atrocity, the enormity of which was unjustifiable.

Rebecca's marital nightmare and her violent physical and mental torture, including her horrific injuries and the downgrading of her conviction from murder to manslaughter, weren't enough to alter the jaundiced opinions of people. To most, unaware of the marital debasement Rebecca had been suffering, she was a cold-blooded murderer who played the lawyer's game and through a fortunate legal loophole had been almost pardoned for an unspeakable crime. Rebecca would have gladly quadrupled her lenient two-year sentence rather than endure another day of vicious abuse and perverted tyranny.

Within the prison, amongst her fellow inmates, she was a heroine of the highest order. Any woman who had murdered a wife-beating, philandering, depraved rapist was protected from prison violence and worshipped like a soldier returning from war. Such twisted adulation for an abhorrent crime, was reprehensible in civilian life but within the walls of prison it was respectable, and she attained a bizarre rock-star status.

There wasn't an ounce of secrecy. The prison authorities knew exactly what was coming into prison and being sent out; it was a way of life. The only secrets they couldn't open, delve into, read or exploit were the ones safely embedded deep within the mind.

From a window no larger than an envelope, Rebecca watched the composure of another dazzling sunrise and sighed for the life she didn't have and the happiness that had always evaded her.

Her cell door clanked open as her mail was slung in and the door shut, as every door in Rebecca's life had. It had to be a letter from one of only two people who wrote to her. One was her brother, remained devoted to his sister irrespective of the controversy that surrounded her. This letter was from her hospital angel, Michael, who had given her the hope and vision to survive the carnage her husband Jack had inflicted upon her existence. It was Michael's soothing words that had given Rebecca the injection of strength she desperately needed. Rebecca had blood on her hands and a prison sentence, but she had been saved from total annihilation; she was still alive to watch the sunrise and feel its glow on her face. Such pleasure in her claustrophobic enclosure was heavenly, compared to the early grave she would have been headed for had she not sliced open Jack's stomach. She smiled to herself and began to read.

Dearest Rebecca

The unpredictability of our lives is inane and frivolous, with the grim reaper only ever one step behind us. Your greatest challenge is to live the life you dream of, before his deathly scythe decapitates your peripheral existence.

You may not be living the life you wished for, however it is still there deep inside your head, it is still alive as long as you can dream. Every day, live the life you desire, give it life with your thoughts. You will survive, and those pictures in your mind that keep you sane will all come to you when you leave prison. There are people out here in the real world, millions of people who are prisoners in their own minds, they don't have freedom. They have given themselves a life sentence of not living, only existing. You might be in prison but your mind is free, and while it is free, so are you. The greatest incarceration of man isn't a jail, it's the walls built within their own minds, inescapable until they take their last breath and taste the fruit of real freedom.

Every day play the movie reel of the life you desire and with each show, you will edge closer to your dreams becoming an everyday reality. Love will wander into your life, unexpected and brash, and with a single stare it will sweep you away to a world of relentless passion, desire and happiness. It will happen, it's your birthright to be blinded by the spectacular sunshine only true love can bring.

Me? It's been almost six months since I left hospital, I've got my last facial surgery to fix my jaw and nose next month, maybe then I'll have the courage to face the world again. The police called the other day and interviewed me about some bizarre suicide victim who apparently had some fixation with me. It was a very spooky conversation, they were vague with the details, almost like they were hiding something. I'm convinced they were trying to insinuate that his suicide was something to do with me. I think they've got me confused with someone else.

Keep dreaming, Rebecca, no one can take your dreams from you and one day they will come true, you just have to believe they will and when they do discover your world, that will be the greatest letter you'll ever write and the greatest one I'll ever read. I look forward to that day with magnificent anticipation.

You are always in my thoughts.
Michael

Rebecca sighed and read the letter a further seventeen times, until each word was emblazoned into her thought patterns, fixating the pleasure of her habitual dreams, methodically playing the same video through the cinema of her autonomous brain.

'Que puis-je faire pour vous?'
The same café, the same Paris street corner and the same waiter asking what she wanted. Rebecca sat at the white wrought iron table, the sun only temporarily shaded from her glistening face by the form of the waiter. This was her dream escape. This was the film of her dreamy life. This was the scene playing in her mind through every twisted trial and tribulation of her impaired, meandering days. Deep inside her heart, Rebecca knew her Paris dream would become reality. It felt so real, the images were so lucid, the imaginary sun actually glowed and warmed her cheeks and every replay lifted her spirits. The radiant sun, the lustrous overbearing stature of the Eiffel Tower, were all part of her performance.

Bruno the waiter hadn't shaved today and was looking more masculine than his usual suave, polished self, but his smile was as sparkling as ever and sent the customary shiver through Rebecca's musing body.

A million splintered cracks appeared over Bruno's chiselled features. The resplendent Paris of Rebecca's mind came to an abrupt clattering end as the shrill sound of her cellmate's voice pierced her beautiful images.

'Stop your dreaming, you silly bitch! Come quick, Dawn is getting cock!'

Paris was annihilated as Bruno's handsome face was replaced by the toothless, weary and perpetually weathered complexion of Rebecca's gritty inmate, Lucy. She grabbed Rebecca by the wrist and forcefully dragged her out of their cell, through the cold, steely corridor and into the steamy communal shower area. There was a loathsome gaggle of prisoners there, laughing and jeering, making the group of thirty sound like match day as the home team scores another goal. The difference was that this swinish multitude of female outcasts were tougher, meaner and more uncontrollable than any crowd of football hooligans.

'This is for you Beccy, all for you darling!' was the excited scream from a butch and toothless prison inmate as she vigorously shook a glass vase the size of a small kettle in front of Rebecca's anxious face. There was an oily black liquid sloshing around the receptacle which reminded Rebecca of a school chemistry beaker of randomly-mixed chemicals.

Rebecca's face flushed with fear and her anguish was replaced with disgust and consternation. The viscous black liquid in the glass flask was not from a scientific experiment, nor was this the beginning of a pleasant alcohol drinking game. This was the beginning of someone's shocking nightmare, one which was about to inflict untold damage upon another human being, scarring them physically and mentally for the rest of their lives.

The contents of the vase were jet black and crawling. It was a hellish congregation of cockroaches, diligently rounded up by the inmates specifically for the ceremonial aggression which was about to occur. The swarming, thumbnail-size vermin were teeming over each other as their hard skeletal shells smashed together, creating an eerie symphony with their customary hissing noise. Rebecca knew only too well what the expression 'getting cock' meant. She hadn't witnessed the degradation for herself but it was prison legend, and the very thought had given her endless nightmares.

Three weeks before, Rebecca had suffered a mild sexual assault whilst showering here. Dawn had touched her inappropriately, and then viciously punched her in the face when her advances were repulsed. For that, Dawn was now about to receive 'cock'. Fracas between prisoners was common and largely inconspicuous and generally ignored, however Rebecca was one of the few prison 'majesties', protected by the other inmates for the glorious crimes she was guilty of. She was a prison prima donna, revered and celebrated by the others and ultimately untouchable.

'For your majesty, the court has deemed a fitting punishment to Dawn McCracken. It is our honour to give her cock for the crimes she has committed against you. Behold ladies, a fitting penance for the slag who dared to cross the line with our prison queen!'

Dawn was restrained by eight burly inmates and laid on a wooden table with her legs dangling from the edge. Two women held down her gagged and bound head, with their hands on her shoulders and her forehead weighing her down with all their might, while the other six were holding down the rest of her quaking body. Without a stitch of clothing on, the only thing her trembling body was capable of was fear. Tears of terror flowed from her swollen eyes. The unimaginable was about to happen.

'Prepare the villain for cock!'

Rebecca's frantic protestations fell on deaf ears as Dawn's restrainers pulled her legs open wide, displaying her pink genitalia.

'Ladies are you ready, are you ready, are you really, really ready?'

Rebecca cried, but the inmates replied with a resounding 'yes!' as they loudly whooped, cheered and chanted 'cock, cock, cock, cock, cock, cock!'

The woman holding the crawling vase of vermin removed her hand from the rim and to the ecstasy of the crowd, shoved it into Dawn's vagina. Three inches of the glass receptacle were inside Dawn as the scuttling cockroaches headed for her soft interior. The cockroaches wanted to escape their glass prison, and there was only one direction to travel, towards the sugar cubes which had been inserted inside Dawn's womb by the eager inmates.

The cockroaches sensed the sugary trail and leapt at the chance of both deliverance and food. Dawn shuddered with pain and terror as the insects fought with each other, nipping their fangs into her soft, pink flesh as they marched to liberation. The crowd were exhilarated.

And then the prison guards arrived and careered into the den of torture, forcing the melee of hungry, depraved villains, apart. They were faced with a detestable sight as all the inmates fled back to the cells and into the prison corridors.

Dawn, unsurprisingly, was unconscious and oblivious to the carnage inside her, her body shuddering as if there was a deathly electric current surging through her flesh and bones. On the floor was the glass vase, it still contained the cannibalised remains of insects, eat by their own kind, while other cockroaches scuttled around, rapidly searching for shelter and safety. Rebecca was the only inmate that hadn't fled, she was on her knees, hateful cockroaches all around her, as she frantically sobbed in disbelief at what she had just witnessed and the new low point her life had plummeted to.

Dawn spent four weeks in the prison hospital. A congregation of doctors and nurses patched her broken body back to normality. The physical scars of her ordeal were healing rapidly, whilst her surprise visitor nursed her diminished confidence and despair with comforting words of endurance.

Deep, deep inside your heart you have to believe you will be OK again. Even if you only have one tiny ounce of hope left that one day you will heal, then you need to hang onto that because that one ounce of hope will get you through, that single ounce will give you a reason to live. Sometimes all you need is hope.'

Rebecca had become Dawn's angel and for every day of her stay in hospital, she beamed rays of hope into her dismembered life and encouraged her crippled body and mind to reanimate back to the living. The consistent goading and heartfelt reassurance boosted Dawn's demeanour in a miraculous turnaround, she was now determined to leave prison and pursue her chosen career in nursing. Life for Dawn McCracken had held so much promise, it was meant to be so much more, before the influences of a villainous group of friends had reluctantly forced her blessed existence off the rails and into a corrupt world of violence and crime.

Rebecca and Dawn's prison friendship blossomed into a symbiotic relationship, every day they reminded themselves about the single ounce of hope that would finally lead them to their dreams, every day they glowed and reflected upon their life mantra 'Live your life and set the world on fire. Come what may, keep your ray of hope alive, keep it deep within your heart, etch it into your life and don't ever forget, every fire started with an insignificant, microscopic spark. Hope will guide you and hope will keep you alive' and every day they clambered closer to the lives they were born to live.

Rebecca's dreams were fuelled and energised. He consistently teased her with the life she knew was out there. Her expression was habitually glazed, oblivious to her confinement and the desperate rigours of prison life. Instead her imagination was sharpened to visualise her ideal world. Every living moment, Rebecca was conscious in her alternative universe.

Today there was a lingering dampness in the air, reminiscent of rainy summers when she had been a child. The torrential rain had subsided and the beaming rays of heat from the spring sun were rapidly evaporating the droplets of water from the white wrought iron table. Service was slower than usual today. Bruno was nowhere to be seen, it was a new waiter and the café was busy. Champ de Mars was teeming with locals and tourists. Rebecca was dressed in a flowing, almost transparent, lemon dress, probably too summery for the temperamental French weather, but she didn't care; this was her dream and she had the freedom to do as she wished. No one could steal these liberated, precious, awe-inspiring moments from her. It was her destiny to live this beautifully-crafted dream.

She closed her eyes and felt the warmth of the Paris sun melting away the minuscule smidgens of heartache and ingrained tribulations her life was so accustomed to. Her prison cell was thousands of miles in the distance, her putrid marriage even further away in her labyrinthine, befuddled past. There was a tactile serenity that only Rebecca could manifest. It was tumbling wave-like through her thoughts, washing through her and sedating her senses. This was Rebecca's definition of pure, unblemished bliss.

The warmth from the sun subsided. A shadow fell over Rebecca's face.,

'Madame, puis-je vous joindre?'

She opened her eyes. Could this soft, pleasant voice be the love she had been waiting for all her life? A rush surged through her body, and her temperature rose as each pore let out a sigh of relief.

The last decade replayed through Rebecca's memory, as she had always anticipated it would, succinctly completing the circle of her dreams, her flashback cavorting through a minefield of torturous memories, from her maladjusted marriage to her lamentable time in prison and the hard years that followed. It had been a wretched decade, mournful and depressing. Time had whisked Rebecca through every imaginable scenario, including some that even a boundless imagination would struggle to evoke. However her ability to escape into a dreamy world of hope, vision and possibility was a sturdy life raft that floated her through the tempestuous sea her life was set upon. She had survived everything fate had harpooned her with, endeavouring to pierce her resolve and drown her into extinction. Her dreams were the power that would drift her to the safety of the island she perpetually craved.

Thud! Rebecca's illusory raft hit dry land and the barbarous sea behind her calmed. As Rebecca stood and glared at her contaminated history from the safety of terra firma, every jaded, impaired reflection of her past sank into forgetfulness, disappearing into the now peaceful waters. One simple question from a chiselled, unshaved face she had never set eyes upon before and she understood the influence and power of dreaming, of simply visualising, believing and ultimately manufacturing heartfelt reality. Through one convoluted turn after another, she was now sitting at the same café, on the same street that branched from Champ de Mars. The Eiffel Tower glorious stood proud, symbolising love, passion and romance. gesture. Even the sun came out to salute the magic Rebecca had dreamt into reality, as she wistfully admired the stranger and translated his broken French into 'Madam, may I join you?'

Her imaginary reply in that split-second of enchantment was 'Of course you can join me, I've been waiting all of my life for this precise moment. I've dreamt you into existence. I've relentlessly yearned for ten long, torturous years, just waiting, fretting, crying but always believing you would come, and here you are my darling prince, here in Paris, here just for me. You are the last section of my imaginary jigsaw. A lifelong picture of how I wanted my days to be, I have now discovered all the jagged pieces and you have converted a scattered, unhappy dreaded and broken life into one of delightful optimism and promising happiness. Yes do sit, hold my hand tight, kiss me passionately, embrace me in your strong arms and never let go, for you have repaired my damaged life and you have made the frightful, excruciating wait worthwhile' Instead, in her own version of scrambled French, she replied in the affirmative: *'Bien sur, vous pouvez, s'il vous plait asseyez-vous'*.

CHAPTER NINE

Mera sakti hai
(Mine is the power)

'I'm not going in, I'm not going in, I'm not going in! I'll kill you,
I'll kill you bastards, I'm not going in, let me go, let me go you
bastards!'

Anywhere else in the world the screaming protestations of a
teenage boy being awkwardly carried by three adults whilst kicking
them, spitting at them, biting their arms like an uncontrollable rabid
dog and shouting lurid obscenities at the top of his voice would
have raised concerned eyebrows, if not prompt intervention from
passers-by. Yet here, literally hundreds of people were indifferent to
the crime unfolding in front of their eyes. In fact many
acknowledged the extraordinary spectacle and did nothing but
smile, almost encouraging what at first impression seemed like the
abduction of a petrified child who was struggling to be free from
his captors.

This wasn't just anywhere in the world; this was a dusty village
in the vibrant city of Ludhiana, in the state of Punjab in India. The
sun was relentlessly beating down, it was midday and the misty
humidity was unbearable, worsening the pungency of the grossly

inadequate sewage facilities and the putrid menagerie of farmyard animals which were rambling around almost every fenced yard, every mud brick-built house. Each household seemed to own a herd of unkempt, yet sacred cows, and each cow was adorned with a cow-bell dangling from a piece of frayed rope around its neck. The air was filled with a symphony of jangles, an ongoing cacophony from the orchestra of holy Indian cows as they restlessly navigated their humble enclosures and attempted to keep cool in the insufferable heat.

Multitudes of people were swarming around a magnolia building, crumbling and chalky but magnificent in its ancient prominence. It boasted an ostentatiously white marble path, dazzling under the beaming sun. The immense arched doorway had the words '*Mera sakti hai*' inscribed in powder blue above it. From within the three-storey structure came an eerie, droning chant bellowing above the noise of the crowd, almost in harmony with the discordant clatter of cow bells: '*Mera sakti hai, mera sakti hai, mera sakti hai, mera sakti hai!*' The same words came, over and over again, hypnotising the air with their monotonous repetitiveness.

The three kidnappers gracelessly removed their shoes and placed them beside the hundreds of pairs embellishing the pristine marble path and entered the building with the screaming child. The sweet scent of burning incense sticks mingled with the sweaty heat of congregated people as the captors and their captive stumbled into an immense room with bare walls. A noisy fan was rotating on the ceiling, stirring the clammy, odorous air emanating from the hundreds of people seated on the floor, chanting and swaying in the immeasurable moist heat. The soporific drone of the crowd and the oppressive temperature mesmerised the hollering child, who stopped crying. They circumnavigated the seated masses and found an area of floor no larger than a pillowcase where they forcefully squeezed themselves in. Sitting down with crossed legs, they gazed in the same direction as the crowd and joined in with the listless chanting 'Mera sakti hai, mera sakti hai, mera sakti hai, mera sakti hai.' They were immediately indistinguishable from the four hundred men, women and children already in the room.

A crackle blared from the four loudspeakers positioned at the corners of the room. At the front of the room was a man sitting in the lotus position underneath a glittering, gaudily-decorated canopy which was suspended from the ceiling with golden ropes. He switched on his hand-held microphone. Everyone in the room was looking at him. He had a painfully skeletal frame, a long, tousled greasy beard and a bald head wrapped with a flimsy swathe of white cotton, resembling a turban. His deep-set, haunting eyes had clearly witnessed more than their fair share of atrocities and burdens, but they spoke of experience and accomplishment. He was enrobed in cool, white cotton cloth. In a rasping, hoarse voice he began talking in his Hindustani mother tongue.

'Welcome people, welcome to Surine Devata Durbar. Salvation will be yours, if you believe in the power within. Mine is the power, mine is the power, mine is the power, mine is the power.' He paused as the devoted crowd continued the chant: 'Mera sakti hai, mera sakti hai, mera sakti hai, mera sakti hai!'

'Yes, yours is the power, you have the power, the power is within you, it's your power, use your power, you have the power!'

The people nodded and intermittently applauded as Surine addressed them again, gesticulating and pointing at petrified individuals with his free hand as he continued his speech.

'I see your demons. I see them breathe their distaste of our holy world as they violate your bodies and strip you of the dignity you were blessed with. God has lost the fight. Evil has prevailed and now follows you like a thick, infectious black cloud, pouring its destructive Satanic rain upon your lives, destroying your lungs as you inhale the damned air of the devil himself, piercing your heart with hateful wrath and consuming your human flesh with their bloodthirsty fangs, contaminating every bone of your bodies with disease, pestilence and hardship.'

The cross-legged herd of followers were spellbound. They let every word sink deep into their minds as they felt their personal devils and demons step back, unable to retaliate in this ecclesiastical, spirited environment.

'That's right. Step away from my people. Be damned back to hell where you belong! Mine is the power, mine is the power, mine is the power, mine is the power.'

The crowd continued their chanting: *'Mera sakti hai, mera sakti hai, mera sakti hai, mera sakti hai!'*

'Come into me, come into me. I compel you to come into me!' Surine's voice became increasingly agitated as he summoned the unholy spirits that were lingering demonically in the room. Children started to cry, frightened by the tenseness of the atmosphere, the sheer dripping heat and the deafening shrill of Surine's grossly-amplified voice. People were fainting. There was no moving air among the denseness of the hypnotised crowd. There was a grinding, rumble coming from all four loudspeakers, high in deep, resonating bass and getting louder and deeper, as it vibrated through people's bones, clattering their teeth and stirring their stomachs.

This was India in the mid-seventies, the most populous democracy in the world. An eclectic, colourful panorama of cultures, religions, gods and beliefs, with one dramatic similarity that brazenly leapt over barriers of ideology, doctrine and heritage – the presence of underlying evil. Fear was the living marrow in every bone and constitution of the hordes. Irrespective of their class, wealth and education, there was always a demonic pestilence threatening to overcome the protection and power of religion and cause unholy, irreparable harm. This evil was conjured by humans themselves to bring untold havoc to others. Black magic and witchcraft were rife in India and created immense fear when combined with the insecurities, fear and folklore of religion. Hypocrisy was contrived by man, subjecting a greater emphasis upon the antithetical rather than the command of God himself, exaggerated evil to bulldoze people towards greater control and consummate worship of religion. People were fearful of the unknown world of the devil, and their prayers and deities were inadequate to keep evil from bubbling into their lives and corrupting their happiness and future, so they flocked in their masses to those blessed with the ability to disarm evil, fight Satan and bring salvation from the hideous creations of the dreaded underworld.

Mental illness, lunacy, derangement, dementia and improperly diagnosed afflictions were often mistaken for voodoo and curses that could only be exorcised by exceptionally talented people. Surine was one of them. He possessed a unique, god-given endowment to battle in the trenches with the enemies from the dark side, enemies who had been summoned by sorcerers and worshippers of god's adversaries. At a very early age, Surine had discovered his amazing talent to rid the world of demons and the damage they were cajoled into doing. His command over evil had changed the lives of ordinary folk and amassed him enormous wealth.

The roar from the loudspeakers thundered and bounced around the four walls and dust fell from the ceiling as the rafters vibrated in unison. Many of the congregation were physically sick, puking on themselves and others. Nevertheless they leapt from within their skins when the noise levels hit an almighty new crescendo. Nervously they continued to chant '*mera sakti hai, mera sakti hai, mera sakti hai, mera sakti hai, mera sakti hai'*, until this was interrupted by a hysterical screaming from the front rows that were closer to Surine. He jumped to his feet and his eyes turned white. Much to the amazement of the crowd, his pupils had disappeared. His eye sockets were wide open, with nothing but ghastly, pale whiteness, intersected with a roadmap of jagged red veins.

'I have you now, I have you now, I have you now,' he chanted. 'Leave here, leave my body and be gone, be gone back to hell!' His voice had deepened beyond recognition, while his body was convulsing, trembling uncontrollably. All the demons had been magically siphoned into his bony frame, sucked deep into his living flesh, blood and organs.

With an almighty jerk, his body went limp and he slumped to the floor. Three of his helpers covered him in sheets of white cotton. He was deathly still. The exorcism had squeezed out all his energy and left him spent. The crowd clapped and cheered. They knew what the unfolding drama signified and they were beyond elated. Their personal poltergeists had lost the fight; they had been overcome.

The legend of Surine had travelled the length and breadth of this colossal, over-populated land, including its indigenous people who had now settled abroad. His stories were elaborated throughout the villages and towns, across religions and cultures. The temporary disappearance of his pupils, turning his eyes pallid white, signalled success in exterminating any demons in his vicinity, and the people were immeasurably grateful for such a miracle. They left the building content in the knowledge that the haunting spirits that had manifested so much destruction in their lives were now banished back to the hell hole they originated from.

About a hundred of the pious gathering remained in the building for a private session of healing from Surine. For them the fee was a year's hard-earned income but a lifetime redeemed. The three adults and the agitated teenager waited for almost thirty-six hours before it was their turn to be seated in front of the godlike exorcist.

'You are indeed cursed. This boy carries the burden of the demon called Mazar. He is standing behind him with one hand on each shoulder, his sharp claws are sunk into the boy's flesh and bones. Mazar is too strong and he refused to enter my body, he will not leave until his work is done. This boy will die a tragic death, but that death will be relief compared to the vileness Mazar will inflict upon him before he dies.'

The adults were horrified and sullen. Surine diligently stared above the boy's head and continued, 'Mazar, I am Surine, Surine Devata. Why are you injuring this boy? Who asked you to curse his life? Speak to me, Mazar. I demand you speak to me, I am the almighty powerful Surine Devata. You will speak to me!'

Surine glared without a single blink, his eyes blood red and wide open. Tears of pain cascaded down his leathery face, speaking volumes about war-torn escapades and decades of satanic conflict. He juddered as Mazar's evil vibrated through his decrepit body.

'Mazar was summoned by this boy's aunt and he will stay until his dreaded work is done. This is the Devil's own handiwork, like nothing I have ever seen before. I will overthrow this baneful curse and send Mazar to haunt the person that brought him to our world, but we must act quickly, Mazar grows stronger by the day and will soon become invincible. The boy will suffer intolerable pain, starting in his gut and spreading like a cancerous tumour. This will be followed by his unearthly, tortured death.'

All three adults tearfully accepted Surine's altruistic offer of deliverance for the petrified boy. The cost was tremendous, but it paled into insignificance compared to Mazar's unholy intentions and the barely-lived life that soon would be abruptly taken.

Surine left the room to prepare for ferocious battle and returned an hour later, wrapped in fresh linen and with another flaccid turban around his head. He appeared relaxed, with a hardened focus in his eyes. In his absence his minions had warmed a large quantity of milk in a battered steel cauldron and placed it next to the bewildered boy. They repeatedly warned everyone in the room not to partake in conversation with Surine, it would be lethal if he broke his concentration, for this was set to be a vicious battle against a hideous monster from the devil's own loins and Surine could not be distracted for a second, otherwise Mazar would have the capability to defeat him and ransack his soul.

Surine was carrying a glistening, jagged sword with a carved ivory handle. His grip was tight, constricting the blood flow to his knuckles and inflaming his hand. He swung the formidable weapon inches above the boy's head, wafting strands of his hair as he sliced the air. In a deep, gravelly voice, Surine began spitting venomous Hindustani blasphemies at Mazar. For ten full minutes the damning verbal abuse filled the room and shook the onlookers. Mazar had been temporarily intimidated. He had loosened his invulnerable grip on the boy. His resolve was momentarily weakened as the vile language spouting from Surine's mouth became increasingly vexatious and insulting.

There was no time to waste. The boy was ordered to take a gulp of the warmed milk. It worked. The boy's stomach erupted as a pungent spray of bitter vomit was expelled from his young body. He was writhing in abdominal pain. The regurgitation was relentless as he was ordered to drink more milk. Mazar was being crushed, frantically spewed out from the very fibre of this young inflicted child. Finally the boy fainted, covered in his own sour bile but liberated from perdition. The three adults carried his limp body away, content in the knowledge that they were not carrying him to his funeral pyre. Another life had been granted.

Surine Devata's reputation travelled the world. Fear of the unknown and sordid tales of demonic destruction were consuming lives and beliefs across the globe. Asian communities were clambering over each other to rid themselves of the nightmares and the anticipated terror of the devil and his worshippers. The children of India were suppressed with black magic. Occultists preyed upon the vulnerability of human ignorance and inherent ideologies, and their only antagonists were exorcists and the practitioners of dogmatic religions. Such denominations were often not powerful enough to vanquish the fear instilled into an entire race of people. Where God failed, exorcists succeeded. Their valiant and audacious quest to combat the wrath of Satan and his sepulchral dominance gained them celestial eminence among millions of tormented people who needed a bodily saviour.

CHAPTER TEN

Milking England

'*Mera sakti hai, mera sakti hai, mera sakti hai, mera sakti hai!*' Once again the monotonous chanting bellowed from every window of the house as the masses crammed each corner, begging for clemency from whatever beastly demons had plagued their infernal lives. The air was moist with the aroma of warming milk, an almost infantile comforting smell, reminiscent of childhood. The white fluid that was innocently milked from bountiful, generous cows served a far greater purpose than simply nourishing human bodies with essential calcium and vitamins. It was the magical elixir for survival against the poisonous, spiteful death and destruction of ungodly demons, haunting poltergeists and an abominable medley of sheer corrupting evil. With incantations from the hands of an exorcist the warm milk forcefully coerced their beastly inhabitants to leave the inflicted humans and descend back to the bottomless pit from which they had originated.

The cows responsible for the milk were not wearing jangling cow-bells. Nor were they huddled in dusty backyards, infested with annoying flies. There were no bony, ragged men draped in dirty loincloths beating them with long sticks and yet heralding them as holy beasts from god himself. These cows were wallowing in the charm of the green English countryside. Indian exorcism had arrived in England.

Surine Devata was sat on a bed in a semi-detached house in the city of Birmingham. His reputation for releasing accursed souls from a hellish demise had crossed continents, and the inflicted were queuing to be in his congregation and vomit out their destructive vileness. Victim after victim paid hard cash and then drank pints of incanted milk before proceeding to clog every waste pipe leaving the house. The stomach-grating bray of regurgitation from every toilet, bath, drain and sink in the house was in discordant harmony with the prosaic chanting. The English summer sun was shining and demons were fleeing Birmingham in their reluctant hordes.

Birmingham was the seventh part of Surine Devata's United Kingdom tour, the final leg of which was ending in the city of Coventry. His final quest in the penultimate city was to treat the burdensome affliction of infertility. A profound soothsayer and resident of Birmingham, skilled in the black arts, had concluded that twenty-four year old Aisha was unable to have babies, not for the usual reasons such as excessive acidity or blocked fallopian tubes but because a venomous, deadly demon had been implanted in the lining of her womb. The cancerous lodger maliciously tore apart her unborn children and consumed them. The demon was growing larger and more deadly as the nutrients from undeveloped babies strengthened its presence and purpose. Its flourishing size explained the excessive bleeding and abdominal pain Aisha was experiencing. The demon had to be exorcised, as his motive was the ultimate demonic objective, to be born as a human and wreak untold havoc upon the human race, devastating the timeless work of god and ravaging the spoils of human achievement. If Aisha's womb remained un-purified, she would give birth to a demon with the will and prowess of Satan himself, and his release into the world would bring catastrophe.

73

Aisha reiterated the story to Surine, who stared intently at the morose beautiful, raven-haired woman. Her tears were leaving a distinct track through the caked make-up on her porcelain skin.

In belligerent tones, Surine addressed Aisha's distraught husband and family.

'Aisha is carrying the offspring of the devil Samnu,' he said. 'It is deep within her stomach and is growing fiercer daily. It is licking the blood from her womb with its poisonous forked tongue and devouring her womanly eggs with its sharp grinding teeth. The prophet who saw the future was right. We have to remove this demonic spawn. We have a right to save humankind from the birth of the devil's son. Satan's shameless desire to rule the earth must never be fulfilled. This will take time and immense courage. I need to be alone with Aisha. It is too dangerous for others to be in our vicinity. It will cost four hundred pounds a day, but you will save us all from the undeniable wrath of the Devil's firstborn, whose aim will only be death and destruction. During the birth, Aisha will die from severe internal bleeding and her soul will be banished to hell for eternity, from where in intense pain and guilt, she will helplessly watch the annihilation her son will cause on earth. It is our responsibility to rid Aisha of this repulsive blasphemy which otherwise will eradicate God's breath and cause indescribable hardship for every living person.'

Aisha and her husband had resigned themselves to a barren, bleak future without children, and now the entire future of the human race was in jeopardy. Without hesitation the anxious family agreed to pay Surine the meagre price of saving their daughter and dutifully protecting God's world from extinction.

Another tray of metal dishes clattered on to the floor. The pungency of rich spices arose from the freshly-cooked food as a hand came around the plush velvet curtains that adorned the inside of the door and grabbed it. For two long weeks Surine and Aisha were isolated. The family, for their own safety, were prohibited from seeing them or even uttering a single word to them. There was deathly quiet, except for the regular creak of floorboards as Surine worked his necromancy upon Aisha's star-crossed soul.

Each step represented another year that Aisha appeared to have aged as she descended the staircase after fourteen days of confinement from the world she was endeavouring to save. Surine's magic had worked. The evilness of Samnu had been exorcised and sent back to hell. Aisha appeared disconnected and bedraggled. She was still confused by the outlandish phenomenon she had been exposed to but she was free and unshackled from the devil and his command over her. More importantly, humankind had been saved from his depraved, megalomaniacal master plan.

Surine had faced his greatest battle and was heading, satisfied in the glory of saving the world from Satan, to Coventry for his final blitz on evil in England. This last port of call and last stance against the nefarious work of the underworld was the family that had invited Surine to England. Their plight had saved countless others from eternal pain and damnation. The young lad central to his visit possessed a vile, twisted and neurotic mind, capable of destroying lives and creating unspeakable havoc. He was yet another distasteful example of the unscrupulous practice of black magic, immortalised by foolhardy people intent on harming others, people who underestimated the evil power they were meddling with by summoning the destructive forces of darkness.

Coventry, painstakingly rebuilt after a severe Second World War bombing by the Nazis, was now at war with an even greater evil than Adolf Hitler. The force of Satan was even greater than that of an insecure, despotic leader of a troubled race. Hitler was no match for God's own fallen right-hand man. The devil doesn't judge creed, culture or the colour of skin; every living, breathing person who has not succumbed to his beastly omnipresence is an adversary to overwhelm and conquer. The quest of Satan, the complete antithesis of God himself, is simply the denunciation of heaven and the outright ownership of every living soul.

In 1970s Coventry sorcery and witchcraft were worryingly rife. The tidal wave of distaste towards the decree of God's heaven was sweeping the country, and it was vigorously prevalent within Asiatic cultures. Surine's arrival in the city attracted the usual swarm of the disillusioned and downcast, nervously foraging for answers to their problematic and disquieting lives.

Michael's parents had searched for the saviour to placate his tortured mind, a final quest in their tiresome journey to rid him of the oppressive trance he was in. It was a frantic and heartbreaking odyssey. They had witnessed their son experience mystery illnesses and horrendous nightmares as he endured a teenage life which was rapidly spiralling out of control. The medical profession gave insubstantial answers and his child psychologist, the much renowned Rosie Devlin, had literally marched him out of the consultation as if she had witnessed the devil himself. Surine's exorcism was their last and only hope to save their son from his final downfall.

Surine's command over the lives of confused, anxious devoted people was immeasurable. They believed he was a guardian angel, a unique celestial spirit, aiding the good work of God, which was often desecrated by his own evil flock in this debased and unorthodox world.

The rampaging teenage hormones contaminating Michael's ability to function as a balanced human being were normal for a child of his age; it was the involvement of witchcraft that had exacerbated his regular youthful angst into a tortuous battle to retain sanity. Browbeaten and doubtful, like all others before him, he psychologically crumbled under the almighty stare of Surine, as his eyes bore into his mind, uncovering dark secrets and yet another satanic possession. Once again, as with all the inflicted before him, it was an unpleasant showdown with reality. Michael's guts regurgitated more warmed milk vomit than could be handled by a teenage stomach. The most unlikely remedy, and yet people were cured of their unholy curses, leaving nothing more than a temporary sting in their throats and a deep, piercing sensation in their abdomens as the satanic vileness fled the body.

Surine's tour was complete. He was exhausted and wearily returned to his home in India, leaving behind a trail of empty bank accounts and contented people who had regained normality in their desperately impaired lives.

CHAPTER ELEVEN

Aisha Khusa

The scream strained her throat as it was forced from her vibrating lungs. She spluttered droplets of blood as her oesophagus felt the rawness of her outburst. Somehow she knew what was coming. There was an imprint of a hand no larger than an orange on her stomach, indented upon her soft skin and stretching it like rubber from the inside of her body, pushing her soft skin to its limits and rupturing the delicate tissue.

All Aisha could do was stare as one hand became two. The pain grew intense as her skin ripped open and spurted warm blood. She had reached the point of mental shutdown. Then the two hands from her bleeding womb appeared, dripping with foetal fluid, to be followed by the rest of the grotesque forced birth. The baby had delivered itself.

Aisha's convulsions turned to paralysed disbelief, her eyes wide open at the being that had just materialised. She reached out to the fleshy, moist prodigy. It was not human. This was not a conception from God's graceful heaven. This abnormality had crawled from the depths of a murky, rotten hell. It was a monstrous face, infantile in its shape but with a bedraggled, bloody grey beard sprouting from its cheeks, underneath the hair and the wrinkled skin of a hundred-year-old man.

It smiled an odious, spiteful smile. Aisha screeched again, but her scream was barely audible as her brain tried to close off the nauseating, repugnance that had just discharged itself from her body. She was unable to move or comprehend her fate at the hands of this deformed beast. It crawled up her body and hovered over her petrified face, its babyish paws pressing upon her shoulders. The filthy, tousled grey beard dangled over her, as the beast stared at her with its loathsome eyes. Its mouth opened to reveal a black pit of hell, with protruding, sharp yellow teeth, showering her with dripping fetid saliva and the rancid foul breath of rotting vegetation.

Aisha was helpless as the mutant baby unfolded its elongated, crimson snake tongue and forced its revolting face upon hers, simultaneously pursing open her lips and pushing the tongue straight into her throat. The serrated teeth sank into Aisha's lips and blood gushed from her mouth as the beastly tongue entered her body and the monster began to devour her exposed and fragile mouth.

Gagging for air and spitting sour phlegm from her throat, Aisha jumped up and woke from her terrifying nightmare. Seventy two hours before, the dream Aisha and her husband had fantasised about for years had become a reality. She was pronounced pregnant. Surine's unique divination had delivered its implausible promise. It had been seven weeks since he had exorcised the unwelcome demon that was resident in Aisha's womb and now she was months away from the child they had wished for. The demonic nightmares were clearly remnants of the foetus devouring Samnu, possibly the imprint of evil he had left behind before he had reluctantly been banished to hell.

Shaken by the distraught images of the monster, Aisha returned to her doctor for her second obligatory appointment, following the revelation of her pregnancy.

'Hello Aisha,' he greeted her. 'Once again, congratulations on your pregnancy. I told you it would happen. I've got your secondary blood test results back and there is something worrying me. I took the liberty of asking for a second opinion and the result is identical. Your blood contains a large amount of poison. It won't affect your unborn child, or at least we don't think it will. However as a precaution we will have to give you a blood transfusion. The poison is not natural and we can't work out how it could have entered your body, particularly as it's not a substance that can be easily obtained. We'll continue to test it further to try and understand. In the meantime, do you have any idea where it could have come from?'

Aisha's reply was abrupt and incoherent as she stumbled out of the doctor's surgery and desperately tried to rescue her spirits from free fall. Back home, she sank into her all too common state of deep, agonised thought. The two weeks of incarcerated exorcism with Surine were a hazy dream, faded memories that bore the hallmark of ten jigsaw puzzles, each with a thousand pieces scattered in her confused mind. Every time a chunk of memory filtered two sections together another anomalous piece devastated the feeble storyline. Nothing was making sense.

The Khusa family were perfectly happy. For them every conundrum and prayer still waiting in the queue for god's attention had been solved and answered, their long awaited infertile misery now history.

Clink, clink, clink, The silver spoon glistened as her mother brought the freshly-made drink towards Aisha, after another unnecessary argument with her husband. Even in these joyous times, fractious exchanges occurred regularly. Aisha's erratic temperament was blamed on pregnancy hormones, and it was becoming one sullen day after another.

Her mother stopped dead in her tracks, as the expression on Aisha's face turned from unsettled to chaotic and distressed.

'You fucking fool, he slept with me!'

One angry sentence directed at Aisha's sulking husband stopped time, hope and belief for hundreds of affected people, as the systematic demise of a corrupt, disorientated world, cold-bloodedly created by a hirsute shyster in a loin cloth, swiftly began.

CHAPTER**TWELVE**

Magical Eyes

'Mum, mum, mum, mum, mum!' The young lad was hysterically bawling. 'Surine's scaring me again!'

It was 1893 and a ten-year-old Surine was chasing his younger brother around their home in Delhi, the capital of India. Children created their own entertainment in India's austere times, money was short, work was hard and kids were humble. At the age of eight Surine had discovered an uncanny trick which he used to charm, frighten and irritate people with. His bizarre ability to twist his eyeballs and make the entire space within his eye sockets turn white as if he had no pupils always created a reaction from his audience. In later years this bizarre skill, now used for harmless fun and teasing, would become his fortune, and in the fullness of time, his destruction. The plan that was inadvertently triggered when Surine's mother made a single, frivolous but life changing statement when he was fourteen years old.

'Our family has witnessed much good fortune, your father has a great job, everyone is healthy and our friends and family respect and adore us,' she said. 'It's probably because you've scared the devil from our doorstep with your magical eyes.'

The mighty empire of India, with its vastly growing population, was god-fearing and devout to the multitude of gods, religions and dogmas that governed, convinced and influenced millions of people. People believed there were equal quantities of holy nourishment and divine power and antithetical evil and damnation intently hovering over their lives. Whenever God was unable to answer prayers, there was always the door of a soothsayer, prophet or psychic open. As fear of the unknown and of dying engrossed people's lives, so did the explosion in belief in the supernatural.

'Arsenic is a chemical element. The main use of metallic arsenic is for strengthening alloys of copper and especially lead. It is notoriously poisonous, in small quantities it will cause severe vomiting and in larger quantities it will lead to death...'

Surine was in a day dream as his chemistry lecturer droned on. He dreamt of the endless possibilities of arsenic. None of his devious thoughts contributed to science or the strengthening of metals; on the contrary, arsenic was to become another elemental molecule in the structure of Surine's twisted master plan.

Everyone can trace the dawn of their beginnings, the thoughts, milestones and experiences that affect and transform their lives. The day, the moment and the occasion of events that change the future always have a precise genealogy. As Surine commanded his first audience of two hundred people who were glued to his hallowed presence, patiently awaiting salvation, his memory somersaulted back to those defining moments.

1915: the population of India was booming, the economy was struggling, people were starving and fortune shone its rare and unlikely light on those who took the boldest and bravest steps. Surine had been bulldozed into a career in chemical engineering, in the same factory where his father and his father's father had built their immense reputations for integrity and productivity. The days were endless and hot. The work was laborious and intense, with the rancid sting of the chemical-infused air harshly impregnating the factory and the entire town. The health and safety of employees and residents was shamefully disregarded. This was the inception of India's industrial revolution, built on the vast experience of its unwelcome British visitors. India was growing at the expense of its people. The vast production of weedkillers in Surine's factory was meeting demand from all over the world, but it was choking the local people as they breathed in the unregulated fumes.

'Surine, Surine, Surine come quickly!' the emotion in his mother's voice was obvious as Surine galloped down the dusty concrete steps. The next-door neighbour was cradling her nine-year-old son, who was clearly in distress, with involuntary muscular spasms and gurgling froth pouring from his mouth. Surine's mother and the distraught neighbour begged Surine to help calm the inconsolable boy. Without hesitation Surine grabbed him and did the only thing he could think of, the only thing that could potentially pacify the troubled youngster. For the first time in ten years, Surine rolled his magical eyes to distract the boy's attention.

It worked. The boy saw the unusual and otherwise perturbing sight and focused directly onto Surine, calming down immediately. Surine's eccentric and blessed ability soon captivated an entire town, and the seed was planted into his Machiavellian brain.

The ingenious seedling of opportunity blossomed and prospered into a mighty oak, feeding on the insecurities of thousands of faithless people searching for answers to indelible questions. Surine had learnt the weakness of human existence, simply that belief was power. If people were convinced that their afflictions and conditions were emancipated, then the sheer potency of their thoughts dominated their insecurities and set them free from their adversities. It was effortless in a world where the majority believed the devil himself was the culprit plotting their untimely demise.

Surine's reputation and bank balance flourished for almost five decades. An insignificant, fragile man, he built a fortune on an inexplicable eye condition, a few well-chosen dramatic phrases and arsenic-laced milk. People believed they had the power and endlessly chanted Surine's infectious catchphrase *'Mera sakti hai, mera sakti hai, mera sakti hai, mera sakti hai'*.

His divine, twisted influence even cured infertility in England. God's only involvement in the charlatan's miraculous ability was to watch him tranquillise Aisha for two solid weeks, with a sedative stirred into her tea, and then physically impregnate her body. This faultless plot showered him with gifts, hoards of cash and limitless sexual gratification, until the clink of a spoon within a porcelain cup of tea exposed the reality, that he was just another fraudster, relying on the curious, gullible and simpleminded nature of people searching for disclosure in a fragmented and befuddled world.

Surine's unique and labyrinthine life tumbled faster than the spirits he conjured and exorcised. There was no demon or guardian angel that could save him from his twenty-five year sentence in New Delhi's Tihar Prison for curing people of their constitutional fears.

CHAPTER THIRTEEN

Tortured Mind

The carnival had arrived. With colour, spectacle and a cacophony of sound, it was a celebration like no other. One by one the performers left their everyday rituals to congregate for the masquerade of the century. There was a razzle-dazzle in the atmosphere as Surine reluctantly opened his weary eyes.

A decade after his sentence had been passed, Surine was too old and frail to fight the inevitable gathering in his mind. For many years he had built solid mental enclosures against the ghosts from his past, knowing they would be the catalysts of madness. The stockade toppled as the baying crowd stepped over the crumbling bricks of his mental fortress. His tortured mind was exposed. Every condemned demon, spirit, monster and child of Satan that Surine had exorcised and banished from earth was now eagerly crowding around his bed. News of his debilitating illness had spread like wildfire in the underworld, as every one of his conquered adversaries was discharged from purgatory to cheer on Surine's final breath of life. The clatter of their hooves, grinding of their teeth and foulness of their cold, deathly breath sent Surine's decaying body into involuntary spasms, while his cursed enemies cheered more loudly. Squelch! Another fang, another fork and another knife were thrust deep into his convulsing body as the demons tore open his ageing, leathery skin to extract their long awaited prize: his cowering, wicked soul.

The scowl of defeat was carved over Surine's dying face, bloodily etched into every breathing pore as he slipped into his new eternal home, carried by the legions of filth, despair and agony, the devil's own spawn, that had waited in anticipation of this glorious moment, the day they would extend the limits of their inbred evilness to this soul they now joyfully had in their possession. An eternity of burning despair, malodorous torture and bitter regret awaited Surine. His legacy on earth was over, but the scars and victories of his reign remained embedded in the lives of hundreds of people, those who had discovered his deceptive existence and felt the stinging bite of betrayal and those who unsuspectingly continued a life of blissful ignorance, knowing a heavenly, talented saviour had graced their lives, saved them from their destructive demons and instilled within them the impressive belief to prevail, exerting their own god-given power from within.

Physically, Surine left nothing of any value. His estate and fortune had been demolished or siphoned off by the corrupt authorities. There were no condolences and no repentance from a family that had ostracised him when his evil scam was unearthed. A short obligatory prayer was read by the prison chaplain as Surine's soulless bones crackled on the scorching funeral pyre in the prison yard. His only material belongings, two letters, one that had been received and one that hadn't yet been sent, went up in smoke as the fire engulfed his skeletal body and suffused the air with acrid darkness.

Dear Surine
For almost ten long and tiresome years I've pondered whether I should write to you or not. I desperately wanted you to know about the legacy you left

behind. I'm the innocent little girl you drugged and raped for two weeks in my own home, night after night, as my husband and parents nervously waited in anticipation downstairs. I'm also the innocent girl who was responsible for your downfall and your life imprisonment.

Every waking day for ten years, I've wished pain, suffering and degradation upon you, hoping that every day brings you untold anguish and regret for the thousands of crimes you committed. I know you've received regular physical pain. It's amazing what influence some money can buy within the walls of a prison that's over five thousand miles away, that was all courtesy of my heartbroken father.

I've been angry for so long now, it's time to let go and let life move on with the biting lesson that everything happens for a reason, even the fact that a monster like you came and destroyed our lives. Ten years has taught me some important lessons, in particular that a bitter and twisted mind can never let a heart be happy and satisfied. Time does heal, but so does the understanding that fate is a long and winding road, with an unknown destination. Even your own fate never calculated you'd have your life and liberty snatched from you and placed into darkness, but that was the price you agreed to pay when you knowingly destroyed the lives and beliefs of innocent people who stupidly placed their trust in you. In my wildest imagination I could never have envisaged where life would take me, and here I am writing to the evilness that butchered my family and yet restored my faith in God's ability to always find a way for those that truly believe in him.

Surine, you left me broken and pregnant without a flicker of hope for my future. My husband left soon after the truth was uncovered, especially as I refused to abort your child, the one you left to grow inside me. I haven't seen him, the man I exchanged lifetime vows with, since that day he walked out of my life. Within two years of your callous actions my parents sadly died with heavy hearts because I, their only daughter, had to move away from home, as the word spread of my pregnancy and the dishonour I had brought into their respectable family. I was blamed for your corruptness. You robbed me of everything I knew, everything I had, and left a miserable, dark cloud hanging over my life. I had no self-respect and my life was crumbling right before my eyes. I lost everything, but sometimes one has to go through that pain of loss to see the beauty of one's life. Sometimes a life of gratitude only grows, when gratitude is all that's left. You literally left me for dead. No family, no confidence, and no sun in my sky, but now my life is ablaze with beauty, colour and a gratefulness borne of the misery you created.

Your son, Sitara brightens every day and forces the sun into my sky with his beautiful smile, a smile you will never see. He has developed a passion for writing. His words are beautifully melting, so natural and from the heart, words you will never get to read. From this day onwards let your ongoing punishment be just one thing and one thing only, quite simply the wonderful gift of your child that you will never, ever set eyes upon, knowing he lives and breathes and knows nothing of your existence. There can be no greater deprivation for you. Sitara, which means star, and my star will glow and eternally light my journey, I will never witness a dark day for the rest of my earthly days.

Surine, I will never forget the sorrow you bestowed upon my life and those that I loved so dearly but I forgive you because from the dark dying embers of what you left behind, is a stunning, glimmering star that will illuminate my world until the very day I die.

Aisha Khusa

Dear Aisha

I can never justify the evil life I have lived and the countless many I cold-heartedly inflicted harm upon, so I won't make that futile attempt. I have indeed suffered physical abusive pain for years and if I had been your father I would have sanctioned the very same onto the monster that damaged my daughter's precious life.

I was strapped to a bed and tortured with boiling water, which was *repeatedly poured over my genitals until there was nothing left but withered, burnt skin, and yet that humiliation and relentless agony was insignificant to the degradation your father continued to provoke and fund. I know and understand that was the bitter sting of fate, twisting its revengeful poison into my unholy life, so looking back, especially after reading your letter, I rightfully deserved every second of the grievous desecration I was delivered. The prison officers dressed me as a prostitute and pushed me into a cell of thirty sex-starved desperate men and watched them beat me, crush me and violate my body, I was repeatedly raped and physically abused for twelve hours, then spent a month in intensive care, after which they forced me to do it all over again.*

I have paid heavily for my crimes with blood, tears and daily regret. My physical punishment has stopped because I'm suffering from a sexually-transmitted disease for which there is no cure. It's been slowly destroying my immune system for almost five years and will shortly take my inconsiderate life.

I'm not proud for what I've done, but I will die a happy man knowing there is a shining star in the sky, my shining Sitara. I'll be eternally sorry, during these, my final days and in my infinite hell where I'm heading, for the harm I caused you and your family. I'm not a good man and I deserve nothing, so to get your forgiveness has kindled my soul. I'm ready to go now. I will leave this earth and accept the retribution that awaits me in Satan's underworld.

Surine Devata

CHAPTER FOURTEEN

The Story of Kai

Vibrant and welcoming, the warmth spread like a new sunrise rising from a dusky, damp dawn, zealously dispersing rays of glowing heat across Kai's cold, lethargic body, gradually beaming onto his grateful face, which was longing for the radiance to inject vitality into his lacklustre presence.

The greeting from the sun as Kai opened his eyes was followed by an intense waking of the senses as reality poured its customary rain over his life. *His* eyes were filled with the warm downpour stinging and blurring his vision as the bitter nectar found a way past his cracked lips and into his dry mouth.

'Ha, ha, ha, ha, wake up you scummy tramp, it's time to have a drink!'

The shriek of laughter from the scantily-clad women faded into insignificance as Kai's audience applauded the spectacle before them. This was street entertainment at its very best, a hilarious portion of slapstick and pathos, all in the theatrical doorway of a prestigious department store, half way through the cold night in central London. The cast of two was simple, but the marriage of two leading men in the prodigious scene was both inspired and imaginative, the desired response of merriment and the provocation of gratitude had been achieved.

Act 1, Scene 1

The hero, gallantly entered the prestigious, gold-leaf decorated doorway of a renowned shopper's paradise. This was London. This was the epitome of class, money and riches, but for Kai, today wasn't a run-of-the-mill shopping trip to squander his immense fortune; after all, he already possessed everything he needed, six layers of clothes, clean dry cardboard and a potent can of the cheapest alcohol his loose change could buy. Tonight was an indulgence. Tonight, for one night only, Kai was going to sleep in the doorway of one of the most decadent stores in the world. Unadulterated luxury, unequivocal chic, Kai was living the dream. This doorway was bigger than most and its usual inhabitants, considering it was rarely free, were untypically absent, so when opportunity knocked, Kai not only answered the door and welcomed it in, he set up his home for the night and was ready to sleep in it.

A friendly gust of warm air was billowing through the gap between the marble floor and the glass doors, and the heat of wealth and materialism was blowing onto Kai. Millions of pounds exchanged hands for luxury items during the day and at night, Kai could almost smell the trail of success left behind and was ready to wallow in its delight.

People had spent vast amounts of money on the other side of the doors and lived exceptionally fortunate lives, crammed with the opulence and self-satisfaction that abundance and prosperity can endow a person with. They were content through the security and comfort of belongings. On the converse, Kai possessed his own immeasurable wealth. As he peered through the glistening windows, his net material worth was below the price of a glass of water sold within the store, yet his supreme level of contentment as he lay in the beautiful arched doorway was comparable to that of the hundreds of people that stepped through his slumbering threshold into a building from which he would undoubtedly be barred. The paradox of fulfilment and happiness at extreme ends of the scale amused Kai as he took the last sip of his drink and drifted to his dream world in preparation for an early morning alarm call from store security, who would violently evict him for the day, to let the hordes in in search of their materialistic dreams into the shop.

Act 1, Scene 2

Enter the villain, perfectly timed and prepared. This stage was his beckoning, an admirable close to the night. He whispered to the crowd 'watch what I can do ladies, hush now, we don't want to wake the tramp before he's had a taste of the good life'. The anticipation was at fever pitch. The cheap alcohol cascaded through his body creating warm mischief, as Kai huddled into his scrappy brown cardboard blanket, dreaming of warm sunrises shining onto his damp, unkempt life.

'Are you ready?' The villain goaded the audience, with bedevilment sparkling in his eyes. The audience gleefully nodded, sniggering and grinning, prodding the villain forward to centre stage, as they themselves stepped back to get a panoramic view of the drama about to unfold.

'Ladies and gentlemen, I bring you the power of warm purifying rain, as it cleanses the filth and degradation on the streets of our beloved London. Behold my weapon of choice, a gorgeous white penis, ready, willing and able to refine and sanitise the dregs of society.'

The villain forced a stream of hot urine from his body, and it rapidly sank through the rotting layers of clothes and reached Kai's skin.

'Ha, ha, ha, ha, wake up you scummy tramp, it's time to have a drink!'

Almost two litres of hot golden ambrosia drenched Kai's sodden life before he realised where the warmth was emanating from. Any attempt to get up was futile, as every endeavour to regain an ounce of dignity from this debased humiliation was counteracted with a vehement kick in the stomach.

'Why protest, dear tramp? You should be begging for this magical medicine, which I'm lovingly parting with, it's a gift from me to you, from rich to poor, from hero to scum, drink and be strong and above all be grateful that I'm willing to share it with you'

The last few droplets from the never-ending dripped onto Kai's forehead. The villain delivered a parting kick, leaving Kai breathless in stomach wrenching agony and the audience breathless in stomach-wrenching laughter.

End of Act 1

Every adversity and forlorn mishap Kai had faced during his tortured life was clouded and buried under a stormy optimism that rushed through his veins, blood cells of bursting positivity that attacked the generally diseased drama of life. The saddest days bore the greatest mental outcomes as Kai's rose-coloured glasses painted the world into a blooming red rose-bush without the thorns of reality. Every challenge was overcome with the hope and cheerfulness of brighter days and the encouragement of life itself. No matter what deck of cards were dealt, Kai always possessed a winning hand, even being haplessly homeless was positive in his mind, compared to the cumbersome burden of having a house to manage and an oppressive mortgage to pay. Kai had a theatrical ability to form beautiful words in his mind, descriptively narrating his life, charmingly titled 'The Story of Kai'. His dream was to be a writer, a magnificent talent waiting to be expressed. However, tonight's ceremonious masterpiece in the rollercoaster melodrama had taken a sinister turn. The frustrations, reckless angst and anger inducing perils of Kai's life had besieged his silver-lined perception and shattered it into a thousand shreds of urine soaked antagonism. His usual array of colourful articulation was paralyzed. His words were unconscious and bereft of inspiration. Every tear that rolled from his swollen eyes drained his natural sunshine and inherent enthusiasm and each one had a memory of pain, bitterness and inconsolable heartache inscribed upon it.

I miss you Mum, why did you leave me? Why did you have to go?

Kai fumbled in his pocket and produced a photograph of a beautiful, dusky woman. He read the words written on the back.

My dearest Kai, no matter what the world throws at you, use it to make your life stronger. There will be rainy days but the sunshine will always return. Think of goodness when there is badness, think of happiness when there is sadness. Then one day, it'll never rain again and the sun will forever shine on your face. I will love you endlessly, you are my sunshine. My love is unconditional. Mum xx

When Mum? When? When? When will the rain stop? When will it go away? When will the sun shine on my face? When? When? When?

CHAPTERFIFTEEN

Unconditional love

'Who's the fucking brat?'

'That's my son, and he's not a brat! Go into the other room Kai, Mummy won't be long.'

'Yes, fuck off brat. Your Mummy is going to get fucked good and proper. I'm sure you don't want to watch, do you? Come on Mummy, get your fucking clothes off!'

'Stop calling my son a brat and stop swearing. Go into your bedroom Kai, Mummy will be with you soon.'

A bewildered ten-year-old Kai, clutching the poem he had brought to show his mother, left the doorway to the bedroom and as ordered, sulked back to his own bedroom and peered out into the night from the fourteenth floor of the high-rise block of flats where they lived.

My mother is my light, my mother is my sight
There is beauty like no other, she breathed my life
And became my all, through thick and thin she is my might.
For every moment alive I will cherish my mother,
Through space and time, through the dark and dim, I will fight.
There is no other, there is no match, my life, my future, my mother
Will always be my guiding light.

'Fuck you, bitch. Don't tell me what to do. I own you. Now take off your fucking clothes, or you and your bastard son will be sorry.'

Kai's mother pushed against the burly grip of her shaven-headed aggressor. She was a quarter his size but she still managed to force him back as his grip on her bony wrists tightened. He momentarily stumbled, but rapidly regained composure on his huge, sturdy feet.

'You're hurting me you fat pig! You don't own me. Now get the fuck off me and get out of my flat and don't ever call my son a bastard ever again, or else!'

'Or what, what the fuck will you do? He is a fucking bastard and you're a little slag who is going to get fucked because I own you, you're my slag and I'm not going until I get my money's worth.'

The multi-coloured skull tattoo on the back of the man's hand swung around to strike the side of her face, knocking her flat onto the bed, which shook with the force of her unexpected landing. She was dazed by the assault, which knocked her senses into another dimension. All she could think of was Kai as she loudly screamed inside, drowning the beat of her erratic heart and the whoosh of her heated blood. She didn't want Kai to hear Mummy's pain.

'D'you want more of that, slag? There's so much more for you, now take off your fucking clothes or Mr Skull is coming back, aren't you Mr Skull?'

The man held up his chunky tattooed hand and shrieked a cartoon voice with pursed ventriloquist lips. Mr Skull was alive and speaking. *'Yes sir. I want to hit the slag. Let me hit her, let me make her bleed. Please can I make the slag bleed? Please can I? Please let me, please sir, she deserves it!'*

'Okay, you win. I'm taking my clothes off, just do what you need to do and leave.'

'Ah yes but it's not that easy now, you little slag, you have to say sorry to Mr Skull too, doesn't she Mr Skull? *Yes sir, yes she does. Say sorry slag, say sorry or I will hurt you, I will make you suffer, I will damage you!'*

'I'm sorry, I'm sorry, I'm sorry. I'm sorry, I'm so sorry!' She was addressing a dispassionate tattoo, as reality spiralled into a surreal blackness and shocked, fearful tears started from her eyes.

'Well Mr Skull, I really don't think that's good enough, I don't think the slag means it, I think you need to show her who is in charge, don't you Mr Skull? *Yes, I do sir. I do need to show her. She needs to understand who is in charge. I think she should cry properly, I want to see her cry. I want her to really cry for us.'*

The fairground was always brimful of excitement, anticipation and boisterous screams of hyperactive energy. It was a beautiful reminder of merriment, of childhood glee and the exultant safety of parents who were never too far away, always waiting on the ground and watching as the rides roared into motion along with the children's adrenalin, animating their young emotions as they feverishly waved at Mum and Dad from the spinning, jostling, reverberating machinery.

Kai's mother was whirling round and round on a demented, insane fairground ride. Teacup-shaped seats spun frenetically, generating a glorious dizzy sensation bordering on sickness. The ride was accelerating almost out of control. She could no longer see Mum and Dad, the maniacal contraption was just too fast. Everything was a blurry haze, a smudged world. She wanted it to stop. She wanted her discomfort restored back to safety. She wanted to see her parents. She knew they were eagerly waiting, but she just couldn't see them. Then there was the pain, an intermittent deep thud in her brain, violently shaking each brain cell with substantial force and the familiar taste of blood in her mouth.

'Is that enough sir? Have I done a good job? Have I taught the slag a lesson? *Yes, Mr Skull. You've done a great job. That'll teach the slag. Now it's my turn and she better be good, otherwise you'll have to try even harder.*'

Mr Skull was unclenched and wiped onto the crisp cotton bed sheet, leaving a crimson smear of warm blood. He had taught her a lesson in the only way Mr Skull knew how, by punching her flesh, her delicate eyes, her pretty nose and the lips that burst and bled so easily. Four almighty, unyielding wallops straight to the face and Kai's mum was instantly transported to the fairground, patiently waiting for the rigmarole to cease so she could run back to her loving parents.

But this time there were no parents waiting, no one to console her. No one to mitigate the gruesome torture of spinning, hurtful pain. This ride was out of control. The blood in her brain gushed from side to side as she reacted to the violence.

In the dark, usually impenetrable crevices of her mind she could hear the distant ripping and tear of her clothes and sense the spiteful mauling of her naked, vulnerable body. The monster's rough, gravelly tongue filled her mouth; she couldn't even muster a choke to expel it as it explored and snaked around her teeth, gums and deep into her throat, forcing her own tongue backwards and inflaming her split lips with his stubble. The endless spinning madness blurred everything in her vision as her futile search for mum and dad continued in vain. A groan from her assailant indicated that his hardened member had been forced into her limp body.

'There you go, slag. You got what you deserved but you're not getting paid, in fact you owe me, slag, you owe me for the pleasure and you owe Mr Skull for upsetting him. Don't you, slag? You owe us and you better have some money or Mr Skull will get very angry and you'll be very sorry.'

Luckily, Mr Skull was satisfied. They had located a wad of cash after tipping the contents of her handbag onto the bloodstained bed.

'Thank you, we'll have that, it was good doing business with you, we hope you've learnt a lesson and understand who is in charge, don't you ever cross us again, you dirty slag!'

Kai stared at his reflection, drowning the debauched sounds coming from his mother's bedroom. Outside his window was a huge dark world. He remembered the words his mum always said whenever he peered across the city. 'My dearest Kai, no matter what the world throws at you, use it to make your life stronger. There will be rainy days, but the sunshine will always return. Think of goodness when there is badness, think of happiness when there is sadness. Then one day, it'll never rain again and the sun will forever shine on your face, I will love you endlessly, you are my sunshine. My love is unconditional.'

Kai meandered back into his Mum's bedroom. 'Mummy, I feel lonely.' And there they were, Kai's longing words filtered through to the fairground, the spinning teacups abruptly stopped and her parents materialised, smiling a welcoming glow of relief.

'C'mon Aisha, it's time to go, Sitara Kai needs you.' Aisha's parents faded into a grey mist as a blanket of cold air shivered through her body and reality returned.

'Come here my baby, come to Mummy, come here my Sitara Kai,' she said. Her body was a gaunt, over-stretched canvas, at breaking point, bruised, violated and overflowing from the discharge of broken blood vessels and the repugnant excretion of another human being, but holding Sitara Kai tightly locked in her arms, came as relief.

'Don't be lonely darling. Mummy is always here for you. I love you endlessly, you are my sunshine. You are my shining star. You are my only reason to be alive. Don't ever be lonely, I'll always find you, I'll always hold you and when I'm not there, I'll be in your mind, hold onto me in your thoughts and you will never have a lonely day in your life. You may be alone at times but loneliness only happens if you let it happen. Always keep me alive in your mind and I will live forever.'

The beauty of mother and child resumed all the goodness of an otherwise uncaring and belligerent world, the way it was biologically intended to be in God's master plan. The wretched disgrace of rape, the wounds and the indignity were almost forgettable in this unconditional affinity of blood-related devotion. Gradually they rocked to sleep on the stained, desecrated bed and blissfully disappeared into their undivided dream world of safety and enchantment.

CHAPTER SIXTEEN

Loneliness

A gyrating globe of prolific life, boundless perseverance and endless energy, generated by the several billion individual beating hearts, pumping blood, vitality and fervour into the immense world, the earth is dynamic, conscious and a breathing soul. It is an immortal phenomenon energised by the fact that no two people are alike. Billions of genetically distinct individuals, all interlocked by one common denominator, all belong to the same human race. Aisha had impressed upon her son that loneliness was a state of mind, and that it was impossible to be physically lonely with the abundance of inhabitants on this miniscule planet. It was a personal isolation borne within the subconscious that created a sense of being alone.

Sitara Kai Khusa had been abandoned at the age of seventeen when Aisha had left her merciless life and died of severe blood poisoning, probably caused by the numerous fiends who had defiled and polluted her body for money. He never established who his father was and his inquisitive mind was always greeted with Aisha's succinctly rehearsed answer: 'Your father is somewhere in India but we don't need him, we don't need anybody, we only need each other. One day I'll tell you the whole story, but today it doesn't matter who your father is and why he's not here with us, all that matters is the blessing of life you have and the eternal blessing you've brought upon my life. That is enough power to be who you want to be and become all that you dream of. One day you will be a famous writer. One day you will find true love, it will save you. It will turn your world upside down. Never, ever stop believing. The day your belief dies is the day your dreams die.'

That day never materialised and Kai never stopped believing that one day he would be a writer and witness the power of true love, nor did he ever hear the clandestine story of his father. He understood there had been unusual altercations in his mother's life, particularly with her family, who had ostracised her. Her father had died when Kai was a baby but both of them, when he was twelve, had attended her mother's funeral. No one spoke to them. They stood alone, almost as outcasts, none of the family acknowledging their presence. All the evidence that Kai had formulated within his mind concluded that his mother had left home just before he was born. She neither spoke of her parents nor did she communicate with them. It was obvious that he was the cause of the unpleasant family rift, which was a consequence of his mysterious and uncommitted father.

For three years Kai had wandered the streets with an unfaltering attitude, an enduring understanding that his current situation was temporary and salvation from the dusty, menacing streets of London was no more than a breath away. Every day he concocted characters and stories for the books he would one day write, often mimicking the plethora of voices and expressions in his mind that would be his protagonists and escape from poverty. Kai's mother had remained the eternal guiding light. Her words of positivity, hope and promise were always a distant beacon, beckoning Kai any moment his spirits diminished. Aisha's words echoed between Kai's ears on a daily basis. They were the beaming lighthouse in the stormy, dark waters of his life.

My Kai, you will change the world with your writing.
Never give up on your dreams.
Bring your own sunshine and light up the dark with your brightness.
Only you can make your life magical, just believe in yourself.

Loneliness never featured in the array of emotions that filled Kai's vagabond days, until today, the day when seventeen years of unconditional love and three years of unsolicited yet idealistic vagrancy had been outflanked by a passing, moronic troublemaker who exploited Kai's impoverished status quo to entertain others.

There was an unfamiliar churn in Kai's stomach, which twisted and turned, harpooning his heart in unfamiliar pathos. Billions of people had been obliterated. Kai's attachment to the world had been dissected. His mind was incommunicado with humanity. Soaked in urine and bereft of optimism, Kai was lonely for the first time in twenty years. Desperation, with all guns blazing, had ridden gallantly into town and barricaded Kai into a downcast corner, clouding his vision and blocking the avenues of optimism that were always so apparent, despite his underdog status in society. Kai was alone, confined in his mental brick prison. There was darkness, nothing but a bleak cloud of dejection and tribulation. He could not see the glimmer of hope that had shined so brightly from his mother's secure and soothing memory. Suddenly, the illustrious beam of confidence that had hidden the dereliction of his inhuman existence had disappeared without any warning, without a second thought, within a few cruel seconds revealing a lamentable, ill-fated life and the infliction of a society that hated his scummy existence.

'Where are you, where are you? You said you would never leave me, you said I was your blessing and you would always stay by my side. Why did you leave me, Mum, why did you go? I'm broken, I'm dying. I'm not fit for this world. I need to be with you. I will come and find you. Then we can be together again. We will be blessed again. I don't want to be here any more. Please forgive me Mum, I'm going to give back this broken evil, wounded life that has done nothing but hurt me. My time on earth is complete. I'm coming to where you are. Goodbye cruel world, I don't belong to you any more, I want to be with my mother.'

CHAPTER SEVENTEEN

Believe in yourself

Every twinkle of every star is a wish someone had made, and tonight the velvety sky was ablaze with twinkles and glimmers of hope, wishes that were just waiting to be manifested in the almighty waiting room of the dark sky, just waiting for the beam of life that would transform them into living, breathing dreams on earth. Personal belief, the greatest generator of power and progress, is the only electricity needed to create the energy required to metamorphose wishes in the sky into earthly validity. This was the most lucrative lesson Kai had learnt in his entire life, as he reminisced back to the very morning he had waved a sorrowful goodbye to a callous, unsympathetic world, to a society that had urinated on his meagre existence and dissolved all his hope, leaving him spiritless and devoid of any self-worth.

There was a carpet of dense smoggy mist hovering above the water, and the gushing and rippling of the waves was the only indication that the river was alive and fiercely flowing underneath the thick morning fog. This place was affectionately known as 'The Death Bridge', as many lives had been whisked away by people jumping from the concrete ledge jutting from the old Victorian railway bridge. Hundreds upon hundreds of souls had flowed into the afterworld with the helping hand of strong currents, freezing bleak water and the fall into a contaminated river brimming with discarded waste and the general filth of London.

Kai was mentally prepared to join the many who had relinquished hope and abdicated the right to existence that a higher command had granted them. He courageously peered downwards as a train rattled above him and vibrated the old joints of the steel and cement construction. The train would be carrying hordes of people in the rat race to their daily lairs to maintain the grind of industry, the churn of finance and the cogs of the commercial world.

Mum, I tried, I really tried but I didn't win, I lost the fight. The rain never stopped, it rained and rained and rained on me and now it will drown me, now it will fill my lungs, take my breath and free me from this jail you brought me into.

Kai closed his eyes and loosened his grip on the cold concrete. His tears had frozen in disbelief, dried from the despair and tragedy of the situation. It was time to be submerged and asphyxiated, to escape from his twenty heartbroken, strained years.

My son, I never left you.

Mother, is that you? Is that you? Are you here?

Kai stepped back. His emotions were somersaulting between incredulity and enchantment. Another train clattered above him with deafening resonance and yet the voice remained crystal clear as it echoed through the dusk of London and pierced every membrane and cell of Kai's jittery body.

Look above you. The sky is full of stars. Every star is a human wish, a wish that was never granted. Wishes that are waiting for people to believe they do come true. If you die today, your stars will stay in the sky, your wishes and dreams will never be. Believe in yourself Kai, believe in you. Be a writer, you can become the best. You have the power inside you. Only you can make your life magical, just believe in yourself. You and only you can bring your wishes to earth. There will be rainy days, but the sunshine will always return. Think of goodness when there is badness, think of happiness when there is sadness. Then one day, it'll never rain again and the sun will forever shine on your face. I will love you endlessly, you are my sunshine. My love is unconditional. You may be alone at times but loneliness only happens if you let it happen. Always keep me alive in your mind and I will live forever. Never give up on your dreams.

The world gushed abundance at Kai as the penetrating force of optimism sliced through his melancholy and despair, setting fire to his perspective on what life had to offer and the inestimable value it possessed. From that very moment every wishful star that Kai had lit the sky with was transposed into worldly reality. The supernal light flooded Kai's distrust in himself and his surroundings and erected a rock-solid castle of intimate conviction that he was uniquely born for unadulterated eminence and his mission was to fulfil that overwhelming purpose.

CHAPTER EIGHTEEN

Romance

'Crush me, control me, crack me, break me,
I belong to you, make my world complete.
Whisk away this pathetic abandoned heart and fill it
With the illustrious gushing of fulfilled, passionate blood.
My birthright is plain to see, I was born only to be
An unwilling partner of sobriety.
My beating cells would rather wither and die, than be without the purity,
Oxygen and fire that belongs within me.
I cried when I was forced from Mother's waiting room,
And I will cry myself to God's waiting morgue, unless
You burn my sickened desire with flawless, doubtless broiling.
Impregnate me with that hysteria, outflank my sensibility,
Corrupt my perception.
Pierce my eyes with magic, wonder and surprise.
Extort my obligations, eradicate my clarity and inject me with
The poison that will build me, create me and ultimately bury me.
I crave true romantic LOVE.
Sitara Kai Khusa.

Love, hope, belief and romance were the cornerstones of Kai's
intuition and a string of stimulating, provocative writing, forcing

the human soul to accept nothing less than its right to enjoy every second of life. His writing was mesmerising and strained the reader's apprehension of this ridiculously short, futile existence, leaving most readers feeling inadequate.

My shattered heart will never heal
The wounds of that desperate moment will signify its demise
It will explode with the anticipation of true bleeding love.
From that glorious moment I will have no need for the prisoner in my chest
It will be freed as the bony cage majestically opens and lets it flutter away.
Captured by the magnetism and splendour exuding from the chosen one,
Oozing its magical force and bewitching my overabundance of flagrant emotions.
I await that exhilarating pilgrimage, the congenial gift available to every Adam and Eve
Until that enchanted promised-land, dances into my world,
For that priceless sublime promised moment of ecstasy,
My heart is impervious in its guardian prison.

Kai wholeheartedly believed in love at first sight, in an acute romantic blindness, overwhelming its victim upon that initial glimpse. There was someone for everyone, not just any random occurrence but someone born for the singular purpose of bestowing another with an all-consuming, symbiotic passion and a deep stimulating desire that was forever, so virile and potent that there was no possible replacement in the event that one of the entwined couple met their demise. A poetic enchanted clinch that would bring about a life of solitude pining for the lost one, or quite simply suicide to join them in the afterlife.

Red blood cells are the messengers of life, carting god's breath, oxygen, around every ounce of flesh and tissue. Kai's oxygen was hope. It energetically flowed through his body, touching, caressing and electrifying the billions of cells that kept him alive. Without hope Kai would not breathe, life would be whisked away in a moment. Hope had been the power, crutch and foundation of Kai's life, from the rapists who had hurt his mother to his vagabond roaming and the notion that one day, the environment would fade into insignificance as his eyes, heart and soul were snatched by the love of his life. Kai's hope had carried him through his rollercoaster life and brainwashed him into fanciful nirvana. He had abstained from relationships in the hope that one woman would have the capability to grab his existence, shake it violently and rearrange his world into an unforgettable mesmerisation, a state of unshakable hypnotism.

'Do you really believe there is a person for everyone but most of us end up with someone who is second best?' The middle-aged woman spoke slowly in a French accent. She looked deep into Kai's dark eyes with a determined, piercing stare, closely watching for his body language and the truthfulness of his answer. Her expression spoke a language of its own. It was harrowed and vulnerable, wanting the right answer but frigid with anxiety that Kai's response might cast a shadow over her life and authenticate what her heart was already shouting at her.

Kai was at another prestigious book signing for his third literary offering, *Make My World Complete,* A heart-rendering collection of short stories and biting prose, posing questions about love and fear and the pseudo-love witnessed by the majority of people who let the fear of the unknown browbeat them into accepting second best. *Make My World Complete* speculated that people live fraudulent lives, blindly faking their love, unknowingly misunderstanding what love means and converting the most powerful phrase, 'I love you', into a pointless and delusional malady, destroying its qualification to stand as the greatest three words known to man and metamorphosing it into a feeble, abandoned, cold-blooded void. Born to move mountains, revolutionise worlds and challenge calamity itself, now dying, insignificant, hollow and a mere parody of its magnitude and intensity. Sullen, drained and left discarded to perish on the lips of a dispassionate, indifferent society.

'Yes madam. I wholeheartedly believe only the lucky few meet the person they were born to love, the one they will discover the true meaning of life with and die in solitude without' he replied. 'The rest of the world will suffer the agony of never experiencing the spark and heat of unquestionable passion. The real tragedy is, they will never know that, because one can't know or understand love, unless it actually happens in the first place. That is the cruel travesty of love.'

The elegantly-dressed French woman took a step back as Kai's words scrawled this ungodly graffiti over her marriage and perception of love. Her heart was in tatters. Her oppressed dread had been realised in one grievous sentence from a bumptious author whose body language fortified every word he spoke, turning his speech into a celestial commandment. The woman was broken, her tears discharged in force to support the deep-seated scars of disappointment. She turned to walk away, bewildered by the philosophising author, knowing she had uncovered the truth from this insightful young man.

Suddenly she stopped and froze. A surge of almighty resentment and years of exasperation rippled through her body as she turned to face Kai again.

'What do you know of love?' she snapped. 'I have been married for two decades to a man who hasn't touched me for years. My body longs to be held. He hasn't kissed my lips for longer than they care to remember. They long to be kissed. His words are not affectionate, nor are they loving, they are commands and are only spoken when he wants something. Yes, I'm lonely, yes I deserve more, yes I crave all the things you talk about, but Mr Khusa, I'm not alone. What was I supposed to do, wander the streets looking for the magic, a magic that may never happen, a magic that may not even exist, in the vain hope that someone is looking for everything I have to offer? No, instead I took the first chance I had, the first opportunity of not being alone. I don't know where my dream partner is, I don't know when he would have wafted into my life. What if the people we end up with are actually the ones we're supposed to be with, the ones that are meant for us? I too want love, Mr Khusa. I want to float on air. I want passion to burn my blood but it's a myth created by people like you. People like you who will die alone, waiting for a wish that doesn't exist. There is no such thing as real love because real love is the reality we end up with, the reality we live with. Now excuse me, I have to go and make my good husband his dinner. I hope you find what you're looking for, Mr Khusa. I truly hope the myth of love finds you. Or will you do what the rest of us have done and just grab the chance of being with someone, rather than being with no one? Good day, Mr Khusa'

Paris, the capital of romance, was the last place on earth where Kai would have expected such a scornful resistance to the genuine meaning of love. The woman's words scorched his sentimental resolve, burning an unexpected hole of doubt into his belief. Her face was singed with agonising discontent, and yet she defended a loveless marriage and a subservient existence. She epitomised all that Kai hated about relationships; she was the antithesis of everything *Make My World Complete* stood for, and yet it surpassed the hapless fear of being alone.

The ocean of life is deep, murky and unforgiving. Waves and waves of uncertainty crash through the dreams and aspirations of people, impetuously drowning ambitions, fantasies and ideals with the harsh realities of the autocratic world. The violent storms of despair and destruction patiently wait to swallow utopian prospects and steer people away from the promised land which they had once believed to be their destiny. Kai's sturdy raft of hope rode the waves of doom, burst through the barricades of mutilated, fragmented dreams which were not powerful enough to fight for their beliefs and now just littered the ocean with crestfallen debris. This raft was not made to sink. It would keep floating, keep swerving through all doubt and restlessness until the thud of land stopped its tiresome journey and brought it safely through the misty, troubled waters to terra firma where dreams translate to substance and aspirations are truly realised.

The vitriol spewed from the disgruntled woman had stabbed the core of magical belief and hope that Kai withheld for love and romance. As he walked away from the extravagant, Paris bookstore, his head took control of his weakening heart and his raft of hope became unsettled.

You will die a lonely man.
No one will love you.
You are a fool. There is no love waiting for you.
You will never be happy.
Your life is wasted, pointless and loveless.

The messages from his mind were a lightning bolt attack on his heart, as his raft continued to drift into the wilderness of an evil, cutthroat sea that had found another victim of human pessimism. His emotions were drowning him in the morose ocean, inhabited by human reluctance to live lives of emotional, physical and material superiority. Loveless souls, aimlessly floating in whichever direction the current forced them to meander, stifled hearts beat by remorseless, victorious minds, into a passionless, melee of pitiful submission.

CHAPTER NINETEEN

Make my World Complete

The unequivocal moment, two worlds collide, commingle and contrive.
A gigantic force unknown to humans, so uniquely vast in size
So immense in sentimental declaration, the sublime celebration
So Herculean with innuendo
So unexpected with shocking exaltation
In that sudden provocation, now so torrid, teeming and free
Fire-powered resolution, there is no solution.
Boldness and purpose twinkle fiery in the soul
Melted together, commanding as one
Dominant and dynamic, gutsy and energetic
Amalgamated hearts, imprisoned in emotional glory.
Ultimate transcendent love, the incomparable and majestic story.

Kai's floundering sunrise was plummeting into the dusky horizon. The words so skilfully and passionately crafted into *Make My World Complete* were transformed into harrowing ghouls, jumping out at him, laughing and mocking at the demise of his emotional prominence and self-righteous mastery in love and passion. Tired, bullying thoughts were crunching and crashing into the walls of his usually secure mind, whirling uncontrollably in a hurricane of confusion, every collision damaging the delicate membrane and denting his resolve.

Kai, you're a fool. You were a fool yesterday, you're a fool today, and tomorrow you will die a lonely fool. Your bohemian bullshit has put a noose around your neck and stabbed you in your ill-advised heart. Kai, you're haemorrhaging, losing the battle. Love proclaimed it would save you, where is it now? Where is love when you're breathless and bleeding?

Kai's self-annihilation was bitter and unyielding. Tears once again were preparing for a victorious march down his lamentable face. They congregated in numbers and cheered each other on with anecdotes from previous crying campaigns. This particular battle was won with ease, nothing more than angst-fuelled dialogue in pigeon English from a middle-aged French woman. The tear army was getting stronger and formulating a war cry for their assault on Kai's melancholy eyes; they all understood their emotional parades were likely to increase in number. It was crystal clear Kai was heading for a temperamental and unpredictable phase in his life, a brand new era of pessimistic turmoil.

Soldiers at ease, stand down, retreat, retreat, retreat!

Every tear heard the command and stopped in their tracks. For the unlucky ones at the front of the entourage, the swell was too voluminous, it was simply too late to retreat. They fell and perished as Kai wiped them into oblivion. There was utter confusion as the watery cavalcade was forced to disperse for another day, when they would make their ceremonious statement.

The tremor sent a shockwave of great magnitude through each strapped log of Kai's raft, as it unpredictably struck land with an almighty titanic clash. Momentarily Kai lost his balance. His knees had weakened with the abrupt and unexpected crunch. He swiftly composed himself, albeit his drifting legs seemed bloodless, entirely feeble, their strength had been siphoned, every corpuscle of blood in Kai's body had brusquely rushed to his flabbergasted face and was scorching his skin with intense, virile heat.

It was beyond any comprehension. The body of an adult operates and stays alive with a miraculous one hundred trillion individual cells. The miracle of life intelligently created by every single one of them working in conjunction with the other, following orders from General Brain, with a speechless, eternal discipline, moment after moment, day after day, until the cessation of life. *Get back in line! I command you to do as you're told! This is my body, listen to me or I will destroy you! Get back in line now or you will be in big trouble!* General Brain furiously hollered his directives, but none of the corpuscles could hear. One hundred trillion cells were quivering to the sound of a voice which competently, with minimal effort, drowned the tyrannical ravings of General Brain. Now there was an authoritative pulse the cells had never heard before and it was beating their translucent walls with a deafening throb. They were powerless, hypnotised into submission. The heat intensified, but this was no fever; this was fanatical, fierce and impassioned beyond the limits set by the dominant brain. Kai's body was in a state of extreme, heightened excitement. His perception and psyche had been injected with a higher aptitude and in the flurry of rampant feelings and pent-up cravings there is only one thing he knew to be immaculately certain, this moment was never to be repeated. His unequivocal moment had transpired.

This is it! This is heaven's unforgettable nugget of dynamite. The unprecedented, inconceivable indulgence granted by an omnipresent authority. I need everyone to pay attention. Let the incandescent blood drench your world. Might is upon us and we must all swim in its staggering influence. I, the beating heart, the ceaseless pump of life itself, hereby resume command over this body. You are entirely my responsibility, under my pulsating jurisdiction. We have one chance to create untold magic, let's charge in unified eminence and precipitate this unique moment of enchantment. Let us conquer and cherish our birthright to love and be loved in return and forever more, live in blissful, ravishing nirvana.

General Brain, without any procrastination, surrendered control to the heart. The five senses of vision, hearing, smell, taste and touch promptly sharpened their ability as the spirited alert woke them from their undependable, slumbering lethargy and fixated their dexterity upon the dazzling prize.

The world faded into insignificance as one hundred trillion diminutive units of Kai's anatomy all palpitated in agreement at one singular centrepiece; a woman. Mesmerised and stunned into collective delight, humanity blurred as the divine spotlight shone in spectacular, sparkling iridescence.

At ten metres, every minute detail was conjuring magic in Kai's enthralled eyes, images of sheer beauty he had imagined a million times, dreamt about and mused about time after time. Now speechless, astounded that such vivid, lucid dreaming had manifested itself into breathtaking actuality.

Her eyes were closed, joining together her delicate brown eyelashes, gracefully intertwined, as the beaming Paris sun glistened upon her perfectly moisturised skin, injecting spring heat into her grateful pores. Sunshine seeped into her face and she applauded it in return with a superior glow, shadowing the power of the intense rays breaking through the clouds. Her mind was projected into a world of deep thoughts, reflections of her bygone days, a life that had reached its ultimate destination by driving her to this precise café in central Paris, with Mr Eiffel majestically towering over her, in his sturdy steel elevation, encapsulating her dreams of a sparkling, destined future. What was her story? What was she dreaming? A thousand twisted avenues, hundreds of broken promises, unsurpassed adversity, abdicated dreams and finally the tortures of her mind, love, life and reality summoned her to this white wrought iron table on this particular corner on Champ de Mars. It had to be today, it had to be now. This was her moment.

Her wavy, chestnut hair wafted in the slight breeze, careered around Kai and transported his aroma into her individual space. Her flowing lemon dress complemented the refinement of her curves, teasingly transparent in the revealing light. It was almost as if she was expecting Kai, almost wishing for her torrid circle to be completed.

Kai didn't move. He was peacefully floating towards the beauty who was fixed onto his pupils, casting aside the multitudes of people bustling and shuffling around him. Then, without warning, he was there right beside the heavenly form, shadowing her from the brilliant sunshine. One hundred trillion cells took a deep breath and prepared to burst with ecstasy. A tornado of emotional magic, wonderment and surprise spun around Kai's brain, bordering on psychotic bewilderment, waves of optimism, amalgamated with spurts of insecurity spiked his mind but amidst the haze of exhilaration, sensitivity and hysteria a celestial presence simply shouted out *'She is the one!'* The time had arrived. Involuntarily words formed and flowered from Kai's mouth.

'Madame, puis-je vous joindre?'

The startled woman opened her eyes, and two worlds collided.

Dearest Michael

This is the greatest letter I will ever write and the greatest you will ever read. In one of the wonderful letters you sent to me whilst I was in prison you wrote:

'Every day play the movie reel of the life you desire and with each show, you will edge closer to your dreams becoming an everyday reality. Love will wander into your life, unexpected and brash, with a single stare it will sweep you away to a world of relentless passion, desire and happiness. It will happen, it's your birthright to be blinded by the spectacular sunshine only true love can bring'.

Well Michael, love wandered into my life, it really was unexpected and brash. It really was a single stare and it definitely swept me away to a world of relentless passion, desire and happiness. It happened! I fulfilled my birthright to be blinded by the spectacular sunshine only true love can bring. I had waited all of my life, and I'd have waited another lifetime to experience the one person destined to hold my hand and break the spell of sadness that has plagued my days. The universe created Sitara Kai Khusa and then faultlessly delivered him to my café in Paris, and from that miraculous moment my life has been showered with more blessings than I ever imagined were possible.

All my dreams are now dead and buried. They are no more than rotting words under the ground because my days are a complete living, breathing dream, they are now alive in the real world. I have no more dreaming left to do, they have all become an everyday reality, leaving me breathless and blind with love. Every sad, twisted, vile moment I have lived was worth it to finally bring me not only the man of my dreams but an explosion of spectacular light such as mere mortals seldom experience. The pain and dread of my past have been swept away and replaced with a beating heart of smiles, gratitude and disbelief that such beauty really does exist in our cynical, second-best world.

You told me to hang on and never accept anything that didn't tear my heart apart with emotions, and for that I thank you with all my being. Your belief, wisdom and vision of love have saved my soul from the mistakes and pitfalls that were waiting to wreck my life and destroy my resolve to carry on and be fulfilled. We were all born to complete the cycle of life and enjoy the sheer power of deep, passionate affairs of the heart. I have done exactly that and I know my final breath on this earth will be one of unadulterated gratitude.

Two months have passed since my (as Kai calls it), 'unequivocal moment' magically happened and I haven't recovered. I never will and best of all, neither will he. I've told Kai all about you. He is a writer and looks forward to meeting you and encouraging you to fulfil your own writing dreams. I have the strangest feeling that somehow all our lives are bizarrely connected, that some way everything that has happened has more affiliation than we will ever know and will continue to shape and create our worlds.

I hope you like the gift we've sent you. It's called 'The Kiss', created by an artist called Auguste Rodin. We saw the actual sculpture here in Paris and it just reminded me of you and the romance you believe in and made me believe in. It had your name written all over it!

I wish you the very best in your new job and I hope London is where you really want to be, doing the things you really want to do. As you've always told me 'Life is too short and it happens whilst you're planning the future', so enjoy every second.

All my love
Rebecca

CHAPTER TWENTY

London

Dear Rebecca

Thank you for the stunning gift, it now sits on my bedside table. It really is a gorgeous piece of romantic artistry. I absolutely love it.

From within the deepest pockets of my heart I have always believed in love, romance and the magic of love at first sight, that 'unequivocal moment' is something that dreams are made of and you really are the first person for whom it became a living reality. Your amazing liaison with Kai has put wonder and surprise back into the air and has inspired me to never, ever consider or settle for second best.

I also believe we were inexplicably linked by spiritual, mysterious streams we have no understanding of, when we first met all those years ago I was blind, bitter and totally ungrateful for the world and you were in a deadly relationship with no value for life or living, neither of us could have ever envisaged our connection and the journeys we would both embark upon. However, what I do understand is they are far from over, considering both of us are beginning yet another riveting chapter in our inscrutable, blessed lives.

Your new chapter is dazzling and full of colossal promise, almost a second genesis from which entire lives could change direction and take an unimaginable course of utter fulfilment, where little else is of consequence. Remarkably, you've even inspired me to strengthen my personal belief in love, romance and passion.

And then there's my latest adventure, venturing to the almighty capital of this country, starting a new life in London, so exciting, yet so full of trepidation, nevertheless a change shrouded in wonderful charm and fated allure, another avenue in the bewildering maze we've created. I cannot begin to put into words how grateful I am for this unexpected opportunity you've created for me. I look forward to working with your brother and will do all I can to repay his kindness in securing my new role.

We have a boundless seam welding our lives together, influencing and powering our symbiotic direction. It is breathtakingly beautiful, awe-inspiring and yet so cryptic. I am eternally indebted to the mystical forces that brought us together in adversity and bizarrely lead us to glorious eminence and splendour.

I wish for love, success and warmth to always and forever shine upon our commingled lives.
Michael

Michael's trademark smile came to a grinding halt; it was almost impossible to curve the corners of his mouth upwards. Through the many twisted turns round which his life had fluidly meandered he had learned a valuable lesson, that a smile had the same meaning in every culture, country and language and possessed the celebrated talent of melting hearts, bonding friendships and breaking down the barriers of disharmony. On this occasion it was physically hopeless. His body was stunned, and the last thing his bemused brain could conjure was a smile. The situation was diabolical, and for once not only was Michael speechless, he was scared. Between the roof of his mouth and his unsuspecting tongue there was the cold, steely muzzle of a gun with a grizzled black finger on the trigger. In the barrel was a shiny bullet with Michael's name carved into it, a bullet that was impatiently waiting to pierce his mouth and tunnel through his head at lightning speed, creating a splattered abstract work of art in a multitude of deathly human colours on the wall behind.

It had been another hectic but successful day in the office, with enterprise, arrangements, decisions and frantic bargaining being telephoned and faxed around the world. A handful of months in London and Michael was already an enthusiastic member of the team, already fast-tracking past Rebecca's brother, who not only was now his trusted colleague but also a friend, one who had been instrumental in assuring the prestigious company where he was an employee that Michael would be an asset to them and their future growth.

Peter's barefaced lie had worked. Three months before Michael had been no more than a heroic name who had encouraged and supported his sister. Peter had never met him. He had only heard divine tales which painted a picture of an extraordinary character. Peter's diligence as a heartfelt gesture towards Rebecca now heralded Michael as a key player in the organisation and on a personal level a steadfast comrade, one Peter desperately needed in the cold, unforgiving capital and assuredly one he could depend on without hesitation.

Dependency was indeed the challenge. Peter's mind, body and soul had developed a scathing and disrespectful attitude towards natural human ecstasy and laughter, turning instead to the manufactured debauchery of mind-bending, delusive stimulation. Artificial motivation had incited his brain into euphoria. Peter was addicted to any substance he could buy, borrow, beg or steal, as long as it lifted him from his doldrums into floating delirium. From an astute, academic professional businessman, capable of monumental deals and prosperous corporation relationships to trudging the wretched streets of London, making shabby deals with sordid people in a dire society of squalor and sleaze. Two contradictory worlds, antitheses of each other, and yet with a striking resemblance in the hedonistic, dog-eat-dog arena of a profitable business institution. It was no more than a street away from the plush comfortable surroundings of high-rise establishment to the gun-toting, underground low-life that peddled powdered misery. Peter was a regular at the den of thieves, dealers, vagabonds and miscreants who didn't hesitate assaulting Michael's mouth, an orifice previously only guilty of sarcasm and a handful of lies, with a loaded pistol, simply because they didn't recognise him. Peter was nervous about today's encounter with the drug dealers' syndicate, as although his income was impressive, so was his debt to the degenerates. Pushing the realms of loyalty and friendship, he had asked Michael to accompany him, but Michael's welcome was less than affectionate. With rapid pleasantries and introductions, the uninvited weapon was reluctantly withdrawn and Peter concluded his defiled transaction.

'Stop right there white boy! When will I get my fucking money?'

Peter and Michael froze, dragged back into iniquity. The man was burly and six feet tall and his scars told horrific stories of anger and debasement. He had appeared from a dark corner swathed in the jangling glory of selling heartache, presenting a picture of pain and retribution.

'At the end of the month when I get paid' said Peter. 'I promise you. I get paid a lot and this month it's all yours. That's a promise, I won't be late.'

'I know you won't be late, otherwise you might just wake up with a surprise and you really don't want the kind of surprise I can send you. Put it this way, you'll never recover from It. So my advice is, get me the money or suffer my nightmare.'

This wasn't a cowering, veiled threat. Each word possessed fangs that tore into the flesh. Long into the evening, the consternation and panic of fierce cold steel in Peter's mouth had been surpassed by the menacing words from the drug dealer. Three stinging words were troubling Michael: 'suffer my nightmare, suffer my nightmare, suffer my nightmare, suffer my nightmare,.' Round and round and round the chilling words circled his imagination. The price he was paying was beyond lethal.

CHAPTER TWENTY ONE

Charlie

A tiny artful bite on the tip of Charlie's toe sent a soft, feathery tingle of sexual delight through her sleeping body, electrifying her leg and instantaneously travelling deep into her damp and lustful femininity. His touch was subtle, so powerful and welcome, silky smooth as it drifted from her feet and swirled around her ankles, the fluidity of surging warm water swishing around her prickly, responsive skin. This was shivering bliss, a stroke so significant and yet so effortless, driving through her veins and fluently persuading her body to secrete its carnal hormones.

Diminutive hairs woke and stood alarmed at the fluttering sensation. Her legs confidently parted in anticipation of the heavenly infiltration. Moist lubrication awaited the penetration of ecstasy and the exultation of man and woman. Sharp, pincer-like bites upon her hot, stimulated thighs were exploding her senses as her limbs quivered with promiscuous rapture and further aroused her dazed contemplation of two bodies becoming a singular, perspiring mass of throbbing euphoria, the ultimate release of wanton contentment.

As he arrived at heaven's doorway, the glowing entrance of human connection, sexuality and reproduction, the intensity of piercing teeth into her dripping fleshy pinkness captivated and inflamed her innermost animal eroticism. Her body begged to be impaled. His tongue violently darted into her. The expectation was unbearable, she wanted him to impregnate her, she was desperate for his weight to pin her curves to the bed and take her.

'Come to me, come here, I need you inside me, I want you inside me. I want you now. Please baby come to me, Peter, I need you now!'

'Honey, wake up! You're having a dream.'

Blurry-eyed and slightly annoyed at being prematurely woken, Peter nudged his frantically dreaming girlfriend. Her body was dripping with sweat, her eyes were swollen with bulging redness and her legs were trembling uncontrollably. Charlie struggled to escape her vivid dream, although she could clearly hear Peter's grumpy protestations. The ecstatic pulses continued to cavort around her exhausted body. The previous night had involved an over-indulgent cocktail of alcohol and stimulants, and the line between unconscious sleep and dramatic actuality were blurred as Charlie attempted to address the situation and ascertain the difference between fantasy and reality.

'It was just a dream, bloody powerful one though' he said. 'You're shaking like a leaf and you're red hot, what the fuck was going on?'

Charlie battled to force words from her mouth. She desperately wanted to respond but her blood was still fighting its way to her stimulated genitals and her brain was deprived of oxygen as her breathing became increasingly deep and tormented. She was still embroiled in the power of her orgasmic dream, bursting with sexual intensity as her quaking body hopelessly strived to catch up with her awakened mind.

'C'mon you, it's all ok, you're back in the living world now, let me take over and give you what you need,' he murmured. He slid closer to his panting girlfriend, her skin clammy with heat, beautiful familiar territory after three years of sex and romance. A walk, a practice, a close knit selection of friends, a regular routine, habitual mannerisms, exhaustive territories, an impregnable home for the human mind, where comfort and normality create security and confidence.

'Drrrrrrrrrring! Drrrrrrrrrring! Drrrrrrrrrring! Drrrrrrrrrring!' the alarm bells were deafeningly loud and crystal clear. The darkest corridor of Peter's mind was now illuminated and bright. Every emotion of dread and fear bombarded his customary mental state. Sickness followed as his stomach churned on a deadly rollercoaster with no safe ending, round and round and round. Restless bile, disgusting and bitter, on a mission to dishearten and forewarn, boiled and bubbled into his mouth.

'What? What? What? What's wrong? Talk to me, tell me what's happening!' he urged her. Charlie's face was frantically contorting and foamy saliva dribbled from her painfully swollen ruby lips. Her tongue curled backwards, attempting to swallow itself as her teeth intermittently chattered and clamped, bloodily biting into the twisted organ of taste, pleasure and speech. Her throat gagged on the red spit funnelling down her oesophagus, which reacted with a brutal splutter, spraying the confused air with discharge from her choking lungs and colouring the white cotton sheets with a rich red spatter of misery.

There was a greater force at play. Charlie began to kick and jostle underneath the duvet, and her body was ferociously convulsing. There was a scream of pain.

Peter's reaction surged into panic mode as his selfish thoughts produced images of overdoses, failing organs, internal bleeding and the jail sentence that would beckon as a result of narcotic abuse, particularly as the illegal substances had been provided from his personal stockpile at his home. This was a disaster, an innocent passenger on a flight directly heading for a crumbling crash, destroying the worlds of many connected people. Charlie's flight was doomed, a collision directed and contrived by Peter, a hapless, ill-fated drug addict for whom life revolved around the brain dissolving high's syringed, inhaled and snorted into his sick and dependent body. Why oh why had he dragged an innocent victim into his wretched charade of an existence? Charlie, his impeccable girlfriend, who three years ago had enjoyed clean, pure blood that happily serviced a healthy, youthful body, had now been reduced to a dumping ground for every impure and squalid drug, potion, stimulant, tonic and pill she could lay her trembling hands on.

'No, it's not my thing, I don't do drugs. I can feel naturally high. I love you Peter, I don't like you taking drugs but it is your life and I won't stop you, but it's just not for me'

'Go on Charlie, it's only cocaine. Everyone does cocaine, just try it once, you'll love it and if you don't, I'll never, ever ask you again. Please for me, just try it once. If you really loved me you would.'

'Okay! Okay! Okay! Just the once, then please, please don't harass me ever again. I'm only doing this because I love you.'

The stabbing movie reel of regret spun around Peter's mind as the words from the fateful evening when he had persuaded Charlie to have her first taste of drugs taunted his already tortured mind. He had knowingly demolished an unblemished life, pestering her demise, watching as the smooth white powder entered her bloodstream via a rolled-up banknote. One swift sniff from her nose and the deadly cargo of carefully chopped and granulated cocaine entered her body with only one solitary intention, to cause havoc and carnage in her naive brain. Charlie's flight had left the ground and had begun its ominous journey of disgrace and ultimate downfall. She was now airborne.

Monotony and chronic routine, the grey matter in Charlie's head, dealt with programmed daily functioning to stay alive. Every meagre cell knew the methodical approach of her thinking and acted out its imperative role with diligence and efficiency. Normally her brain produced a pleasantly shy personality, her creative imagination and a contented, blessed life. Day after day after day her brain cells performed their role with accuracy and bliss.

Today, the sky looked different, the brain cells hadn't noticed. Why would they? After all they had functions to implement and comply with. Their mundane routine was unavoidable, unstoppable; even the quiver of the forthcoming storm didn't distract them from their responsibilities. There was a spasmodic shudder, a fiery quake, vibrating the insipid composition of the industrious cells. Reluctantly, they stood still, alerted to the unusual tremors bouncing and reverberating off the gelatinous walls of the brain. To their utter shock and bewilderment it started to snow. None of them had witnessed such a spectacle. Huge white, globular crystals were sparkling above them, briskly heading their way, as the sky turned a tumultuous shade of agitation. This was no ordinary fluctuation in weather, it was no ordinary snow, this was cocaine, and its arrival was the beginning of the corruption and exploitation of normally virtuous brain cells.

As the crystals landed they instantaneously saturated the permeable walls of Charlie's petrified grey matter as the hysteria of the unknown turned to infuriated partying and the hypnotic tango of illegal stimulation. Charlie's brain was fuelled with irrational enthusiasm as her brain cells throbbed with energetic delight, rippling with excited palpitations. For twenty minutes the insane fever took control, as abnormality crushed convention and a trillion separate units of Charlie's head had the frenzied orgasm of their lives, knocking them into a state of drained exhaustion, crippling them beyond comprehension and summarily craving the exhilaration of cocaine again. Lift off had been a success but this plane was destined for a deathly crash-landing. The safety of controlled, passive living was eternally derelict.

'We have the right to party, we want to party. You woke us up, now you need to feed us. Party, party, party, party!' The chanting was relentless. Peter had breathed life into a dormant beast, one with a ferocious, indestructible appetite. Charlie kept on climbing, and within thirty surreal months of that inaugurating snort of white plague he had broadened her dependency and restricted her reasoning.

Peter looked up and there she was, at least ten rungs higher than he had ever climbed. Charlie's tumultuous affair with these brain-scattering drugs had injected her with a tawdry courage to keep rising and bluntly refusing to peer downwards at real life barking its establishment from below.

'Crunch!' The weight and distress of Charlie's visual convulsing and wrenching splintered Peter's already unsettled rung and he crashed to the cold, harsh punch of reality.

'Charlie! Charlie! Charlie! C'mon girl, that's enough now, get up, you're going to be fine.'

A multitude of mind-bending, reality-twisting, eye-popping substances had rushed through their veins many times over for many years, but this was one expression Peter had never witnessed. The wide-eyed shock in Charlie's eyes was pure vivid death. Charlie's arm quivered, bending round and clutching a handful of blood speckled duvet, but the five-tentacle extension to her arm didn't resemble the hand Peter knew. Her fingertips were a decayed, black colour, throbbing with coagulated disease and more reminiscent of a corpse than a young woman.

She threw back the cover with all the might she could muster, and it wafted onto the floor. That precise second heralded the metaphorical opening of Pandora's-box and a malign tidal wave of horror and loathing.

Blood trickles as each word, picture and associated emotion is carved into the human memory. Seconds, minutes, hours, days, weeks, months, years float by; there's no stopping the fluid motion of time. Relentlessly the components of life tick away the futile existence of humans, from that ethereal light that exchanges the sublime darkness and safety of the womb to the concluding new dawn that stampedes into existence, celebrating a life that has terminated the blessed duration it was granted. Inflexibly etched into every membrane of enterprising tissue is a selection of events spanning the hallowed years of life, happenings that utilised their outright emotional power and dimensional adequacy to shape, deform, metamorphose and challenge every waking moment following the unwilling exposure. The birth of a child, the death of a loved one, from happiness to sadness, from exhilaration to depression, from ecstasy to despair, every individual has their own collection of succinct etchings that are eternally inscribed into every beating corpuscle of their presence and ride high in the charts of thoughts, sentiments and tremors that will prolong the last human breath long enough to relive those moments of extremity, the precise infrastructure that moved mountains and altered the landscape of life.

Peter's face flushed to paleness, the drab, meaningless hue of a corpse. His befuddled brain and distraught heart registered the vile potpourri of emotions that would curse his final twitch of human breath.

The grisliest imagination would have drawn a line at creating this abnormal spectacle. Human experience and censorship would have met its limits and been unable to conjure such a repugnant nightmare of revulsion. This was an original chapter in the obscene and never seen. Peter froze for what appeared to be infinity as the intricate details maliciously carved into his sanity.

Charlie's eyes were now forcefully shut, a gesture of kindness from her psyche, the only protection now available to her from the unmanageable convulsions. Her protestations jumbled into gargled moaning as her teeth clamped and chattered. Peter was not spared such an amnesty. His eyes were painfully dilated beyond the level any snorted white substance had ever managed, fixated on the ugly, nauseating drama unfolding in his own bed.

Charlie's legs were harrowingly swollen and marred by numerous volcanic skin eruptions, each one oozing a distasteful mixture of blood and yellow pus. The big toe on her right leg appeared to have no tip to it and was discharging a crimson weeping of blood, as the fullness of her body quivered and exacerbated the deadly flow. Each bruised and bleeding wound was deeply beyond the thin covering of flesh and centred round twin punctures of her skin. The abnormality of the abysmal writhing mess of legs, the limbs which were usually passionately wrapped around Peter's torso, were desperately clenching together, involuntarily attempting to limit the destruction being caused.

In a futile attempt to control Charlie's trembling, in his state of disgusted shock, Peter grabbed her thighs. She violently shook her head and vomited, as he parted her legs and uncovered a lower level of hell than they were already visiting. An entire, unimaginable disaster unfolded. Peter and Charlie were not the only inhabitants of his bed.

The uninvited monstrosity was brownish-grey, with a lighter belly and a scaled back, two feet long and with a coffin-shaped head with slit-like evil eyes. The sudden movement of her legs prompted the scaly beast to release the pink fleshy, inflamed mounds of

Charlie's vagina and at lightning speed show its discontent at being threatened and disturbed by opening wide its purple-black lined mouth of pitiless torture. It flexed proudly over its prey before scurrying over Charlie's thigh and scuttling off the bed, to vanish somewhere in the bedroom. It was a venomous black Mamba snake, one of the deadliest snakes known to man, and it had been biting and gorging on Charlie's body, in an intimate, moist place which for three years had been visited only by Peter.

'I know you won't be late, otherwise you might just wake up with a surprise and you really don't want the kind of surprise I can send you, put it this way, you'll never recover from It. So my advice is, get me the money or suffer my nightmare.' A whirlwind of disgust and pandemonium was swirling through Peter's dumbfounded psyche as the words from the dealer of death appeared as burning subtitles, highlighting the appalling state of his girlfriend and the crashing thud as he hit the bottom of the bottomless pit he had been falling into since crawling into the despicable world of drugs and the creatures from the dregs of society that provided them so easily and so uncaringly.

Peter's waking moment shunted his ghastly reality into slow motion, almost as if his brain wanted revenge for the years of damage it had silently withstood, being frazzled and depleted with every substance created to destroy its purpose to think, act and learn. Tears poured from his eyes as the snake poison careered through Charlie's feeble, surprised veins transported it to her vital organs, rapidly removing their ability to operate her already beaten and battered body. The woman Peter had pursued, courted, loved and perverted was paying dearly for his inability to pay the debts that had provided their unprincipled persuasion to use narcotics. The promise of retribution from drug-peddling gangsters had been fulfilled. Their debt was being paid through human misery, and undoubtedly it still didn't clean the slate. This was merely a grisly warning that deadlines for repayment had been disrespected. Peter still had an obligation to repay the beautiful highs he and Charlie had willingly bestowed upon themselves, knowing their inability to pay the moneylenders and drug dealers was akin to carrying an undetonated bomb which would ferociously tick on as the boundaries for repayment got closer.

The crescent of curvature glistened with sharpness as its still, steely grin pierced Charlie's buttery soft skin two inches below her seeping naval. With a fluid motion the blade continued in a straight line until the cut was between her limp breasts. Her skin, muscle and fat parted like the Red Sea, proudly displaying the contents. The grim reaper peered in and to his delight noted that her liver was tarred black with the filtered carnage of relentless desecration. Her stomach was decorated with multiple oozing ulcers, simultaneously crying out their leeching pain and the greatest jubilation, her heart was begging for mercy, as the Black Mamba's venomous saliva lacerated its membranes and polluted the oxygenated blood it had been designed to pump.

It was time to say farewell to life and embrace her waiting death. The reaper stood cloaked and proud at the stupidity of self-destructing humans. With his scythe still dripping poisoned blood, he extended his skeletal arm and placed his long, bony fingers around Charlie's frantically-beating heart. Dark hell and almighty squalor glowed from his destroying grin as he looked at his victim and relished her pain as it further fuelled his perseverance to squeeze the life and soul from her desperate, surrendering body. The crimson fibres from Charlie's heart enveloped and cushioned the Reaper's knuckles as he stretched and tugged the muscle of life from her body and gratifyingly held it high, relinquishing life with one final spurting beat her heart conceded to mortality. Charlie was dead.

In tray

The brain has a thousand pieces of information, wisdom, thoughts, emotions whooshing into your in-tray, mostly subconscious education from a world that transmits signals for every second a breath is leaving your body. The most complex filing system known to humankind is the one we're blessed with, filtering and segregating between 'critical' and 'frivolous' and a hundred levels of importance in between. There is such magnanimous intricacy that an identical portion of mentally-ingested information can be assimilated in a thousand different ways by a thousand different people. Even pondering the extremities of death and destruction has a multitude of discrepant responses where such a threat is grasped purely based on the experience, mental state and general attitude of the recipient.

Peter's unique psychological in-tray processed threatening data with a trenchant and inappropriate nonchalance, borne of a disrespect for the futility of life itself and an existence addled with the false and misleading confidence of illegal substances that debased 'critical' to 'frivolous', with a heady misunderstanding of human vulnerability.

It was payday, a perfect opportunity to pacify his vicious money-lender and detach himself from the hair-raising intimidation of 'suffer my nightmare', but Peter's mischievous in-tray was dealing with such aggressive input with an alarming whimsy as he arrogantly let the deadline pass by a full twenty-four hours, instead opting for an immodest pat-on-the-back for himself and his equally noncompliant girlfriend as they injected, drank and snorted through their evening with a belligerent cocktail of drugs and alcohol.

Another morning in the office and the familiar sight of Peter's empty chair and real in-tray overflowing with unopened communication and pointless breached deadlines didn't raise any eyebrows, until the radio which dampened the monotony of the office bellowed out a poignant news story, sending shudders through everyone in Peter's office.

'And in other news, a man in his thirties was found naked and badly beaten in the doorway of St Bartholomew's Hospital in the early hours of this morning. His condition is described as critical. He is currently in intensive care, awaiting an emergency operation to repair his fractured skull. Police have confirmed that the body of a woman in her twenties was found in his flat after he called the emergency services to report the incident. They have not confirmed the cause of death. The police are waiting to question the man, who may be unconscious for some time.'

Peter's aggressor had fulfilled his threat, his menacing nightmare had become Peter's lamenting reality. The only redeeming feature of his unadulterated tribulation was the swiftness with which Peter was abducted from his flat and beaten to a bleeding, cracked pulp, immediately after he had called the police about his violated girlfriend. The impromptu kidnapping and subsequent violence upon his body quickly extracted the horrific image of his dead girlfriend, poisoned by a ferocious black mamba which had been slipped into their bed by the cold-blooded assailants.

Fired from his prestigious job and slung into a rehabilitation clinic with the severity of a police investigation hanging over his head and money-lenders, despite their nightmare actions still wanting their investment returned, Peter would have found his in-tray stacked with a noxious avalanche of conflict.

There was no escape from the loathing he had willingly manufactured, nor the malady he had single-handedly bestowed upon Charlie, wrecking her life and pillaging her final breath on earth. Imagination was the only barrier blocking the wonderful journey of life, and it was now littered with the bloody carnage of wasted lives and irreparable damage. The horizon had disappeared, replaced with horrendous pain, regret and melancholy and his only salvation was the one thing that had led him onto the path of destructive pandemonium. In the absence of any psychological fulfilment, a strong dependency on lethal drugs was the only way to unravel the contortions of twisted reality in his decaying mind.

Dearest Rebecca

From the finest words ever to be read, to the saddest letters I've ever had to write, we have exchanged both ends of the spectrum, from success to tragedy. Our lives are speckled with love, laughter and sun, only to be continuously overshadowed by destruction, tears and darkness.

I'm sorry you couldn't be at Peter's funeral. Rest assured I was there beside his coffin, but more importantly than that, during his last few weeks, I was able to share some of my life with him, some of the inspiration that has flickered a liberating light at the end of the dark, isolated tunnels that I have encountered throughout my journey. I'm just sorry that wasn't enough to change the course of his destructive life.

Tomorrow the sun will rise, another day will beckon and life will go on. Keep your brother alive in your heart and his life will never have been in vain. Remember him before the plague of drugs devoured his life, remember him as the only person from your family who didn't ostracise you in your time of need, the only person who gave you courage and helped you through your own dark days.

I'm going to leave London. Working at this company is not the same without Peter being here and I'm going to pursue a temporary role in Thailand. I also feel I owe it to Peter, considering it was an overseas opportunity that he created but couldn't fulfil himself because of his dependency. Being away from England and separated from all the people I know will certainly help to reawaken my ambition and perspective on the things I truly desire. If nothing else, I expect it'll be another adventure that will inspire and illuminate my life.

Goodbye for now Angel, I hope your romance continues to blossom uncontrollably and every day you wake to a life of love, wonderment and gratitude.

Michael

Dearest Michael

I'm not even sure how to begin telling you of the grief that has saddled my life. You referred to me as an 'Angel', but I truly believe I'm an angel of death. I have brought destruction into the worlds of people and now I have a second name that will be inscribed into my gravestone, this time my own blood, my own brother. I understand I had to defend my own life and brutally take Jack's but I will confess to you, I am totally responsible for Peter being driven to his sad and untimely demise and I don't know how I can live with that guilt and his blood on my hands. This is God's retribution for taking Jack's life, for destroying one of God's creations.

While I was in prison, even though I was a local heroine for what I did to Jack, times were very hard and the only way to buy total security, comfort and well-being was with 'prison currency'. Prison currency only came from the outside world and had to be smuggled in by guests. The lowest denomination was cigarettes, the highest value item that could be used to barter and buy with was drugs, the more powerful the drug the stronger its value within the prison. It started with Peter bringing me cigarettes. The guards knew it was going on but always turned a blind eye. Everyone was receiving discreet packages from their guests and as long as the guards had an easy life they really didn't care. Then on one particular visit Peter saw that I had a bruised face. Skirmishes were common within that scum hole, so to help me buy greater protection, Peter increased the value of currency he smuggled into the prison, from cigarettes to illegal drugs in one easy step. The more he brought me, the easier my life got, however Peter wasn't just bringing me the illicit substances, he had been tempted to try them himself and because they were potent concoctions, he became an addict and even when I left prison he continued travelling on the road to nowhere and his addictions soared out of control. The drugs, potions and pills instilled within him a heart-breaking contempt for his own life.

Michael, the equation is simple. If I hadn't killed Jack then Peter would be alive today. He helped me and got caught in a lethal trap. I have my brother's blood on my hands and there is nothing I can do to bring him back. I'm sinking fast and running out of air. I have but a few breaths left within me and I know those will be snatched away if the inquest into Charlie's death proves it was also drugs related.

So you see, I write to you with a heavy heart and certainly not as an Angel. Yes, I have found the love of my life and every waking day I am grateful for that amazing miracle that Kai has created but life hands me goodness and happiness with one hand and indecency and sadness with another. I'll never quite understand the vast complexities of our short lives but I do understand that the dividing line between victory and defeat and conquering and surrender is a very fine and blurred one.

Please take care in Thailand and I really do hope it opens new doors, *gives you inspiration and some wonderful experiences. I'm really pleased for you and what you have achieved and I'm delighted you're pursuing circumstances that Peter initiated, it's a lovely tribute to his memory.*

Rebecca

Tortured Love

You swathe me in flowers, deep crimson blooms that nourish my forgotten senses.

You deluge my pores with the sweetest ambrosia and alluringly thrill my flesh until it surges with moisture and glowing sensitivity

But then you isolate me with dread and you torture my soul, you nail my heart to the floor and burn my resolve, tarnishing it beyond human recognition.

You assuredly palpitate me back in time when love evaded my being.

When I was lost without hope, a wandering pointless nothingness, lonely and abandoned.

Why do you torture me, when I love being embodied by love?

When I love you so, you drive me low.

Why do you tear my sanctity and embellish my nights with breathless agony longing for what I haven't yet lost?

Why do you crown me queen and then banish me from your throne?

You repair my bleeding cuts, then you savage my heart to shreds and bleed me to death, leaving me alone.

Why does love torture me?

Why when I am its most obedient servant, pupil and master does it destroy the walls it builds?

Why does it devour my body with orgasmic ecstasy then rape my mind and mutilate my beating embodiment.

You make me brave and I face the world, then you make me cower and drench me with fear.

You overwhelm me with a torrent of fire and then devastate me with revulsion and obliterate my desire but I am still here.

Love Replies:

Fool! How will you ever understand my eminence if you don't understand my torture?

Value the crucifixion of your heart for I will pummel it into emptiness.

I will violate its petty rhythm.

I will desecrate that wretched red flow that carries your breath.

I will dishonour your legacy to love and be loved.

I will make it a martyr for your sullen memories and then proclaim triumph and celebration when your adoration for love meets death.

Then in that victorious moment of love's languishing downfall,

In those lamentable tears of bitterness and grief, of remorse and dismantled belief,

I will be the resurrection, I will be born again.

I will bring you flowers in every hue.

I will colour your universe with enchantment so true.

I will kidnap your senses and eradicate your memory,

Your heart will flutter to dreamland and be fanciful and free.

Love will conquer your mind and become your obsession

It will levitate your soul and be your glittering possession,

And while you blissfully float, I will persevere and gloat

For I have a plan, I have a plot, I have the power to execute your creation.

I will torture love and kill your infatuation.
I will snatch your prize and conjure its demise,
This is my future, this is my destination.
There will be pain but you will cherish the gain.
For the love you crave, you will eternally be my slave.

Sitara Kai Khusa

It was a vile disease, rampaging through each corpuscle of blood and passing on despair and desperation to each cell as it guzzled all human life from her decrepit body. This was the worst death anyone could suffer, because it wasn't death at all, it was a living, breathing death. She was alive but she was dead. Rebecca's guilt and dishonour at the collapse and darkness she had brought to Peter's life was devouring her flesh, wasting her away and turning her once fanciful utopian existence into a doomed struggle to see through a single day without desperate tears and a consistent cloud of depression and mortification enveloping her mind and body. There was even a poignant icing on the already fetid, crumbling cake, she didn't attend the funeral, warned off by a family that despised her, a family that saw her as a rancid plague, a murderer who had cold-bloodedly massacred her own husband and stolen away her own brother's life. Rebecca had dulled any shine her family had buffed in the entirety of their family tree, it had been blighted forever. She was an embarrassment, an illness. She was a world of sadness that rained upon everyone who had an ounce of the same blood. A tree that once bore promising fruit, one that would carry a legacy of love, success and fortitude had been chopped down, destroyed in its prime. Its once young, plump offerings, with such promise and potential, were now riddled with the malodorous stench of hopelessness, a sordid contamination spread by Rebecca, the stifling dark cloud of misery, her parents wished had never been conceived, she was a criminal waste of human breath.

The equation of life

Endless, mind-numbing, soporific hours, simply trying to calculate and fathom the necessity of their future importance. What is the point? How will it help? How can I use this information? What on earth does it mean? I don't need this in my life. Mathematical equations that only the gifted few understood and calculated with ease but even a smaller minority understood the relevance of, in the general landscape of life.

$$A + B = X$$
$$X - B = A$$
$$X - A = B$$

And yet in its simplest form the equation signifies balance. It works because both sides are commensurate and that the corresponding accuracy of each eliminates each other, creating equitable harmony. Either side of the equal sign is symmetrical, albeit the antithesis of each other, thus demonstrating the prerequisite and veritable equation of life itself.

Balance has to be restored to counteract and fight the many travesties, challenges and tribulations of life.

Every occurrence in the lifespan of a person attaches itself and fiercely parasitizes human emotions. Cutthroat, insensate fangs that burrow into our flesh and relentlessly desire sustenance, directly stimulating and stirring those little twisted, barely understood, mountainous feelings we are all blessed with. Emotions that continue to nourish, explore and generate associated sensibility, every second of our lives, until the final breath leaves our lungs and our bodies are void of soul.

Rebecca's life was in titanic disproportion. Peter's untimely death, the vile and bitter angst of her family, her disreputable time in prison and her degraded life with Jack, her frightful see-saw of life was heavily laden on one side, with no counterbalance to even out the burdensome load and create composure in her dispirited existence. The only light that twinkled at the end of a boundless and pitch dark tunnel was Kai. It was faint, but with a careful squint, it was still visible through the immense, dreaded darkness that devoured all the light in her life. Kai had become the only force that Rebecca could rely upon. Her once-in-a-lifetime unequivocal moment remained the glitter in her darkened skies, the little sparkling star that was dependable and sturdy. Kai was a formidable crutch that upheld her crippling mental challenges.

Another sunrise dared to appear as another day bellowed from the dark of night. This was a fresh opportunity to welcome life and continue the lengthy sad farewell to the past. Rebecca jostled in her bed as the five seconds of serenity, the confusion of waking, the false sense of security, as the mind registers its existence to the world, blurred her reality and once again she forgot the burdens that were devouring her mind. Five seconds of distracted bliss and the mountain of melancholy landed upon her without warning, crushing and eclipsing the erroneous five seconds of joy into distant oblivion. The latent curtains were drawn in her eyes, even before she had a chance to let in the light by drawing the material, physical ones. Desperation and regret were sprouting eternal roots within her wavering soul, the imbalance of her life was getting heavier on the negative side, rapidly negating any positive light that was daring to push through the murky fog of dejection. A copious injection of unmitigated encouragement, enthusiasm and anticipation was the only antidote to anchor the slope in Rebecca's perception.

CHAPTER TWENTYFOUR

Unequivocal Moments

It glistened with a knowing pride as a spark of sunshine beamed through the wavering curtains and bounced from its glassy exterior. It shone into Rebecca's pupils with a gleeful confidence. There was a flicker of exhilaration as Rebecca's inner voice shifted its customary, downcast outbursts to shouts of 'this could be the answer', 'you could be waving goodbye to the past', 'it's time to walk out of the rain and waltz into the glorious sunshine'.

The prominent glass jar, one foot in size, with a copper lid, appeared to smile and whisper 'open me', 'open me', 'open me, 'open me' in a sanguine tone that instantly lifted Rebecca's heart, muffling her mind and putting her waking five seconds of bliss onto continual, uninterrupted repeat. What was this jar of magic that Kai had left for her? Through bleary eyes Rebecca read the hand written label; 'Unequivocal Moments'. Two words instantly conjured magic, wonder and surprise, cramming her arteries with a gush of heart-beaten blood and blooming her skin with an auspicious gleam of anticipation and elation.

Sunlight shone in your hair and it magically glistened
You smiled and it melted my heart and I thought about it all day

You called me beautiful and my heart skipped a beat

You tasted my coffee for perfection before you brought it to me

This morning you had that look. The one that says more than a million words

I smelt your warm skin when you woke and didn't want to leave you

Your eyes sparkled bright and lit my day up

You made me think of my future with optimism and wonder

I wondered about my self-belief and I realised it came from you. You have made me believe in ME

You came home early because you knew I was there too. I love your gestures

You whispered I love you, while we made love

You kept your arm around me all through the night

I heard you sigh as I held you close

There was emotion in your voice when you spoke of our future together

Just the way you fluttered your eyelashes at me

You squeezed my hand tighter while we watched a horror film

I heard you talking about me to your best friend, saying how lucky you are to have met me

I thought about you all day and missed you for the five hours we were apart

I fell asleep next to you and the last thought I had was a prayer to say thank you for being in my life

Everything happens for a reason, you have become my reason to be alive

I named a star after you and every night I look up at the sky and thank MY lucky stars that you came into my life

You looked at me for that extra second and I felt my heart take an almighty leap'

You asked me to read you a poem, then you listened intently

I have become to realise I am your blood and I have the responsibility to keep you alive, come what may

I haven't taken even a sideways look at another woman since the day I met you. You are the only woman in the world I ever want to set eyes upon

Today, you simply looked ravishing

The black, lurid clouds hovering over Rebecca's tortured life shattered into a million sparkling droplets of shimmering magic, saturating her skin as they penetrated her languid body and strategically dissolved, washing and exterminating every molecule of dejection and misery. The equation of life had been restored.

Nothing had the capacity of repairing the past, overhauling her regret or laundering her debased memories. However, a large jar titled 'Unequivocal Moments' brimming with hundreds of carefully folded and dated pieces of paper simply inscribed with daily thoughts, emotions and observations that had happened to Kai, creating his personal unequivocal moments, tipped the balance of burden plaguing Rebecca's days. With each unfolding, tears of utter gladness poured from her eyes. The incantation of dreary gloom had been obliterated.

The sheer gratitude for today's sunrise irradiated the nightfall of yesterday and decisively rearranged Rebecca's perception of tomorrow. The world was exuding brightness, drowning her sorrows with optimism and quenching the lifeless negativity that had become her daily, humdrum routine. Rebecca had been mentally enriched and had psychologically advanced disproportionately, with the facile twist of a lidded jar. Once again her eyes and mind were open and susceptible to the outright grandeur, artistry and rapture of life.

CHAPTER TWENTYFIVE

Bangkok

'Did it have to be you? Why you? I trusted you. I let you into my home and this is how you repay me. Just get out!'

The shockwave of the hefty blow to the side of Somchai's head splintered his skull, even before the gossamer-thin skin covering it had time to release the profuse bleeding. The effect was identical to tapping a hard-boiled egg with a spoon to crack the shell, magnified a thousand times – effortless and easy. The sound of the connection between the wooden baton and Somchai's greasy, perspiring temple was reminiscent of hitting a cricket ball high into the unsuspecting sky. Thwack! And then stillness, as his brain immediately stopped the match. This was game over with one single, weighty swipe of the bat. It was done. Life had been swept away into the unknown sea of death, never to be witnessed again. There was no tomorrow, not even a momentary awareness of the assault. Just a bleak unconscious darkness and a distant echo of vibrating pain as every human function failed and obliterated.

Somchai slumped to the floor, crushing his nose against the dusty concrete and frightening the creeping assemblage of insects into a myriad of erratic directions.

The assailant continued to forage around for his prize, oblivious to the cadaver and now more reluctant than ever to censor his noise as he rumbled and searched through Somchai's belongings. Elated with his plunder, he nonchalantly stepped over the body and made himself scarce as the sweet scent of death silently infused the musty air and alerted the enthusiastic flies to the appetising corpse in their vicinity. It was another inconsequential, random death in downtown Bangkok. The invertebrates glided into the crime scene in their hordes to savour the casualty and pay their dutiful respects.

Twelve hours later the enthusiastic insect community was heartily feasting on the defenceless and rapidly decaying body. Their irreverence to the passed life was astounding as they burrowed into Somchai's hardened skin and laid the eggs of decomposition into his dead flesh. Every creature completing Somchai's circle of life was consuming a burdensome existence, one that even in its bleakest days had never anticipated this debauched and bloodthirsty demise.

The son of a solemn factory worker from one of the millions of impoverished Thai families, Somchai had used his limited education to carve a significant career in engineering, which was quite a feat in the smoky, burgeoning, industrial capital city, Bangkok. Earning a steady income in Thailand's crumbling economy was an impressive achievement, particularly as it was not in Bangkok's notorious tourism industry. The streets were oppressive and cutthroat. Somchai's income had protected his family of eight from the thieving, angry vileness of his poverty-stricken co-residents of Bangkok. Life was at times weary and arduous, but Somchai and his family always had shelter and food on the table and in comparison to the miscreants of society prowling the filthy, mercenary streets, their life was enriched and contented.

Superstition played a hefty part in Somchai's life and on numerous occasions the intuition borne of his beliefs had rightfully chosen faithful and auspicious roads to travel, particularly when life had halted at a crossroads. He was never one to feel regret, and today was proving to be different and riddled with morbid contradictions. Somchai had rejected his reliable gut instinct and travelled down a dangerous metaphorical road, wholly neglecting his perception and sixth sense. Life for him and his family had just crashed and crumbled in a second of indecision and spontaneous reaction.

Dentistry was usually the lowest priority with people in Thailand, particularly poorer people who had to give precedence to basic everyday essentials. Somchai's teeth were unusually strong and healthy and going to the dentist was a luxury that he annually allowed himself. This was one of the indulgences he could afford, having a regular income. In his semi-conscious, delirious state of mind Somchai was vividly hallucinating. The dentist freakishly towered over him, almost afloat in the air, his bloodstained white coat adding to the menace of the scenario. Somchai lay there numb and helpless as the dentist forced open his mouth with the cold steely forceps and began to rummage ferociously around his mouth, repeatedly clinking Somchai's teeth with the heavy implement.

The dentist spouted a satisfied laugh as he grabbed a tooth and started to yank it from side to side, tearing the delicate gum and roots with all his might. The pain from the tooth forcefully gyrating and loosening in its protective cavity shot a lightning bolt down Somchai's convulsing body, as if it was attached to every pain receptor he owned. His entire body was vibrating uncontrollably as his hallucination became a harsh reality more ludicrous than the floating dentist.

The blinding sun was intermittently blocked by the shadows of staring faces, men women and children looking down with fixed glares and worried frowns. Their mouths were moving, performing obvious words but the sounds were muffled by an incessant whirring and the deafening sound of traffic. Somchai's fate had taken a grotesque twist. A spur of the moment decision to stay at work thirty minutes longer than usual had counteracted his intuition to leave at his accustomed departure time. That fatal choice meant fiercer, faster rush-hour traffic, people eager to reach their destinations in the calamity of Bangkok's highways. Those thirty insignificant yet poignant simple ticks of time brought a goliath tanker careering into his path. The immense collision catapulted his flimsy car twenty feet into the air and make an almighty crash landing as it crumpled onto the dispassionate concrete embankment.

Somchai hovered back into his comatose world and was greeted by the deranged dentist. He had removed the clattering teeth and was injecting calming sedatives into Somchai's arm. Somchai felt a sense of relief. His dream world was steeped in reality in comparison to the bizarre happenings in the real world of the Bangkok rush-hour. He was almost pleased to be back with the dentist. This was calm in contrast to the catastrophe outside that Somchai was struggling to comprehend.

'Sir, are you OK? Sir, can you hear me? Sir, shall I proceed? Sir, you need to agree.'

Somchai drifted in and out of consciousness and finally slid into blissful oblivion as the powerful sedative numbed his agitated body, then he smiled and forced an agreeable nod. The world watched in wonderment while the authorities cleared the bloody carnage and separated Somchai from the tangled debris of his entwined car. Road engineers, firemen and doctors worked hastily to ensure the congested road was passable allowing the frustrated Bangkok inhabitants to go home to their families, a pleasure Somchai's family would not be privy to on this cursed and fateful evening.

CHAPTER TWENTY SIX

The Signs

Blinding neon light, huge clearly-defined letters, totally impassable and impossible to ignore. Every step, every corner, every avenue, every moment of indecision radiant with an incandescent sign, emblazoning your world to point you in the direction of success, your greatest potential and most luminous possibility and always in the opposite direction of failure, unhappiness and agony. A faultless universe, a perfect existence, where only exceptional, jubilant things happen, sparing us our inherent backbone ability to make judgements, decisions and act accordingly. Nothing to be learned, no mistakes to be made, no regrets, just the right direction every single day, relying on your simple competence to read the beaming, lustrous signs in your daily path.

'Don't go to work today.'

'Take the next road.'

'Tell her you love her.'

'Make that call, he needs you.'

'Change your flight.'

'Tell your father what he means to you.'

'Apply for this job.'

In the congested highway of life the directional signs have been removed and erected deep within each living person, with the undervalued yet acute talent to read, understand and rely on them to drive our lives into the stream of least antagonism and maximum harmony. That intuitive, involuntary habit is transmitting beams of guidance from the moment your brain has learnt to apprehend thoughts and emotions. Wherever intuition guides you, irrespective of how bizarre and unlikely the direction is, you will undoubtedly have been rescued from a notably counteractive situation. Listen to your heart. It miraculously beats the drum of predestination; there is every chance it will lead you into misfortune and sorrow. However, you'll never know what trajectory it emancipated you from.

Somchai woke and immediately recognised his surroundings. He was in a hospital bed. There was a fierce rush of awareness as flashbacks of his encounter with the tanker lit up his cloudy brain. The pain from beneath the stiff, beige, stained cotton sheets was insufferable, but compared to the torturous bulldozing Somchai was subjecting upon himself, even his wounded misery saluted the superiority of his mental beating.

Why didn't I listen to my intuition, why did I stay at work when my heart told me I was wrong? Why didn't I go home on time? Why was I so stupid? I'm an idiot and I deserved all I got for not listening to my inner voice.

Over and over again Somchai battered himself, his self-deprecation bringing tears of burning regret to his eyes.

Enough, you fool. What is done is done. Time to go, my family awaits me. No more self-pity, I need to get out of here, I've been an idiot but I'll make up for it and work harder than ever. From now on I will always take my heart's advice.

With renewed vigour Somchai switched his anguish to immediate action with a sharp yank. A stray droplet of blood splashed onto his face as he energetically pulled out the embedded tube from his bruised arm. His body was screaming 'No!' but his unfaltering mind was singing a contrasting song. He had things to do and places to go. There simply wasn't the time to be pitifully lying in hospital while the uncaring world carried on living. Ignoring the protestations of his aching limbs, Somchai grabbed the edge of the sheet and hitched it to one side. Apart from the all-consuming sting of relentless pain, something didn't seem right. Somchai was witnessing an obscure sensation, one which through his complex and variegated life he had seldom experienced.

There came an almighty, heart-stopping crash. Somchai was hit with an unimaginable force, capable of shifting a mountain. From that second, life took a sinister turn. This was a collision that changed Somchai's world.

His expression froze in time, too traumatised to even blink. A million images of despair and hardship vividly presented themselves, impervious to the diabolical scenario or to Somchai's ravaged heart and tortured mind. A verbalisation was seriously needed, a release from the cumbersome distress. There was a loud announcement rumbling deep in Somchai's jumbled stomach, a chain reaction of bubbling bitter acidity. It gathered colossal pace as it climbed up through his body, up his constricted, breathless oesophagus and out from his mouth, the only way his brain could conjure the necessary reaction. A deafening scream pierced through every wall of the hospital as Somchai finally broke down and liberated his exasperation, angst and utter disbelief.

Both his legs had been amputated. There was nothing from mid-thigh downwards, no knees, no ankles, no feet and no toes. His limbs had been severed through living flesh, blood, bones and cells left at the roadside for vermin to feast upon. Somchai was inconsolable. He wished life had just been whisked away in the crash rather than to have this forlorn disability thrust upon him.

Life rapidly tumbled into an endless dark hole, a chasm of no return. There was no end to the darkness that fell upon Somchai and that of his destitute family. One callous decision from a medic at the scene of Somchai's crash nonchalantly stole his future, with no regard to the barrenness and hardship that would rain upon his snatched life. Time and tenderness would have untangled the twisted metal wrapped around Somchai's legs. The sixty minutes saved by slicing his body in half meant the destruction was cleared faster and the traffic moved on to normality quicker. Even the blade-happy medic who had taken Somchai's delirious nod as authority to do an immediate roadside operation returned home satisfied, not because another life had been saved but because the Bangkok traffic had been shifted and his job had been done.

One elementary reaction can have a domino effect on the lives of hundreds of people, unaware people who could never comprehend the result, a result borne of a simple thoughtless action. Life is a complex jigsaw puzzle with millions of pieces moving in every imaginable direction. Each piece fits into the next, but the virtual floating sections of the enormous, inexhaustible jigsaw can alter entire landscapes and produce thousands upon thousands of infinite variables. The incalculable outcomes patiently bide their time waiting for decisions, behaviour and activity. Unlike a real jigsaw puzzle, where a piece is cut and shaped to fit the entire picture, without which it will be incomplete, the never-ending jigsaw puzzle of life shapes the ongoing picture based on the piece that is placed initially. It's simply a progressive chain reaction.

The roadside medic added a lethal segment to Somchai's future blueprint. Unknown to him he substituted the picture of Somchai's personal jigsaw puzzle and fabricated an alternative existence, a grotesque reversal of fortune summoned by Somchai's refusal to hear his own intuition and leave for home on time.

Regardless of success or failure, happiness or sorrow, life or death, one global effect stays constant, never faltering, never ceasing, determined in its procedure and always on schedule. Day follows night, brightness follows darkness. The sun rises day after day, shining and dazzling the earth with its lustrous, splendid beams of life, light and warmth.

There was little left in Somchai's life to be grateful for as the sun burnt his back on the dusty, insect-infested Bangkok pavement, where he was a stinking inconvenience, a dirty scavenger, a worthless scourge of a listless society. Crawling along the streets with his empty trouser legs trailing behind him, begging for charity, was the only option left for Somchai. Every other door of opportunity, fortune and possibility had been apathetically slammed shut in his face, cruelly chopped away. The tourist trade remained his only hope, relying on their sympathy for such a pathetic creature dragging himself through the bustling streets using his worn fingers and broken fingernails to pull his impaired torso forward.

The crush of fate was ruthless as shopkeepers would hurry him along from their precious shop frontages. A grimy cripple was far too much competition for passers-by who would rather stare at the creeping unfortunate than glare through the shop windows. Sticks, stones and hefty kicks were all utilised in the anti-Somchai arsenal. Regularly battered and bruised, the unkempt stench of his decaying body and rotting clothes would attract a carnival of insects to his mutilated face. They felt superior to this slithering vagrant as they attempted to bite his skin, crawl into his mouth and nose and relish the thought of his flavourful, moist eyes.

CHAPTER TWENTY SEVEN

The Tourist

The ratio between callous assaults from merciless shopkeepers and sympathetic generosity from the tourists was at least twenty to one. For every twenty abusive actions Somchai endured at the hands of unfeeling locals, there was one saviour who would leave coins jangling in Somchai's rusty bowl, which on exceptionally hot days burnt his lips as he pushed it along the pavement with his mouth. Western tourists were horrified by the sight of Somchai crawling along the vile streets of Bangkok, begging for mercy as the majority of people stepped over him, around him and sometimes onto him, with the disgust they would show when seeing a pavement littered with dog excrement. In reality, Somchai's social standing on a street scale was marginally below the excrement. The cockroaches and the excrement were avoidable and removable, but Somchai was always there, foraging for the kindness of strangers.

Another tourist leg appeared, recognisable by the shiny leather shoes he was wearing. Another opportunity beckoned as Somchai crawled towards his potential bounty and tugged at the stranger's linen trousers, pushing his tin bowl forward for a compassionate monetary reward. The tourist recoiled in abject horror at the unexpected pull of his trousers, the reprehensible vision of Somchai and the shocking aggression the creeping vagrant endured from the local shopkeeper, who then maliciously beat Somchai with a stick the size and shape of a cricket bat. The tourist hastily scuttled off, while the shopkeeper, disgruntled at losing a potential customer, angrily went back inside his shop, shouting obscenities. Somchai slumped into his bowl, drowning the few coins that were in it with blood gushing from a fresh wound and his bitter, downtrodden tears.

'Hello, I'm back. It's a brand new day full of opportunity,' the sun rose and relentlessly shouted at Somchai. He couldn't actually see it, since he and his family had been forced to move into a spare room at the back of an unkempt, filthy restaurant. There were no windows, just dark dungeon-like despair, but Somchai knew the sun was outside inviting him to grace the pavements one more time. Somchai crawled through the restaurant kitchen, the stench and disease-filled alley, the barking dogs and the vermin towards his morning resting place opposite one of Bangkok's many exclusive, opulent hotels. It was the perfect position in which to catch the residents leaving for their day of Bangkok tourism.

Ostracised as he was from everyday normality and the twisted emotions of an uncaring society, fate had taken Somchai to hell and back, but left Satan's claw print embedded deep into his bleeding heart. Even that hellish disqualification and drawback couldn't infringe the powerful aptitude of destiny as another chapter of Somchai's life miraculously unfolded and his story altered in the space of one blisteringly hot morning.

There was a swift, dusty whoosh as a shoe kicked away a vulgar and determined black beetle which Somchai was struggling to keep from his face. His only physical defence was blowing air from his pursed, cracked lips. It scared away most insects, but this one was clearly daring and hungry, and the odour of stale, bloodied facial meat was far too tempting.

Somchai dared to look up and see who his courageous Good Samaritan was. The shoes were familiar. Somchai invariably recognised footwear, as they were always in his field of vision from the pavement. He was instantly overwhelmed with dread and fear, and mentally prepared himself for another beating. The freshly-polished black shoes belonged to the tourist Somchai had encountered the previous day.

The wounds from the day before were still raw and painful and Somchai's face was bruised and swollen. There was a crick in his neck, probably a splintered bone. The ferocious thwacks the shopkeeper had dealt him had been hefty enough to floor a strong man, let alone a pathetic, scrawny cripple. Nevertheless, the divine outcome of this second extraordinary encounter made every brutal violation from the embittered shopkeeper seem worthwhile. The tourist forged a benevolent friendship with Somchai and his impoverished family and whether borne of sheer guilt, considering the motive of the shopkeeper's angst was to protect him from Somchai's advances, or simply compassion for a fellow human being, the money the stranger gave him made a huge difference to Somchai's life. His family now had money to improve their debased dwelling and pay for some essential medical assistance. The tourist had also commissioned an English-speaking Indian waiter from the restaurant to keep a congenial eye over the hapless family and regularly report back their progress.

CHAPTER TWENTY EIGHT

The Waiter

'Inderjit, table six, table six! Why haven't you served table six? They've been waiting twenty minutes and they're complaining, get over there now or you'll lose tonight's wages!'

'I'm on my way, they're lying. They only arrived five minutes ago.'

The air was infused with the aroma of rich spices and the kitchen was alive with Indian sub-continent banter and the unmistakable rattle of cockroaches scuttling around the grease and curry-stained floors. The wealthy customers were all foreigners, residents of the plush local hotels. 'The Days of the Raj' was one of the most popular Indian restaurants in the area. Inderjit Phal was having an objectionable evening serving the many diners clambering into the air-conditioned restaurant from bustling Nanchong Road.

'Inderjit, table six are now complaining about your bad attitude. You've just lost tonight's income, now sort your attitude out before I deduct money from tomorrow's shift too,' snapped the manager. Inderjit was incandescent with rage as he stormed into the kitchen and fiendishly stomped on the first four cockroaches that materialised from underneath one of the ovens. He delicately picked up the crushed vermin and there was a squelch as he pulled the dead insects apart, removing the majority of their robust, shiny black shells.

'Is this the curry for table six?' he asked. The cook guffawed loudly and nodded.

Inderjit dropped the crushed insects into the pot of golden, bubbling curry, spat into it twice and vigorously stirred the unusual ingredients until they dissolved and were overpowered by the steaming garlic, turmeric and tomato.

'That'll teach you to complain about me and get my wages docked,' he sneered.

Table six hungrily ate the spiced concoction of chicken and squashed cockroaches which only five minutes before had been meandering round the kitchen, with Inderjit's own bitter phlegm. Pungent Indian spices heavily season and mask a multitude of cooking sins, but struggle to camouflage a fragment of shell from an unfortunate, simmered cockroach, notably when it rebelliously lodges itself between the teeth of an unsuspecting diner.

'Inderjit, Inderjit get over to table six, they've found something in their food, they're not happy!' shouted the manager.

An indignant complaint followed, with a threat of reporting the incident to the authorities. The choking, nauseous diners from table six shouted their revulsion and spluttered their way out. The chef was petrified about losing his job and without hesitation confessed the origin of the ingredients. Inderjit was fired from his role as head waiter and now faced deportation back to his native India.

With no income and absolutely no means of sustenance, Inderjit was seven days away from becoming homeless and roaming the streets for food and shelter, drowning in an unforgiving sea of hazardous depravation in the lurid alleyways of ailing Bangkok.

Desperation now filled Inderjit's befuddled mind. Becoming another of Bangkok's filthy down-and-outs was not an option. His thoughts meandered from affirmations and progressive solutions of finding work to ideas of destructive, villainous and ignoble acts of lawlessness.

Fear resides deep within normal, law-biding humans, a powerful buttress against nefarious crimes, short-cutting traditional methods of hard work and determination to wealth, success and lifestyle. Without fear, random acts of law breaking would be more casual and widespread, leading to the lowering of the prevailing standards that are commonplace in Western society. Criminals are simply more daring than everyday folk. The desperate state of mind injects a dynamic and omnipotent venom against fear, converting it to a previously clandestine, boldness and gallantry. The poison of desperation was trouncing every molecule of fear, judgement and sensitivity in Inderjit's body as his evil, liberating master plan briskly took shape in his mind. The potential outcome of his escapade clouded the comprehension of any repercussions and possible confrontations during the breach of sanity, logic and empathy.

This was simply common debauchery, a heinous crime against another human being and an acute contradiction to common sense, knowingly entering another person's property with the sole intention of stealing their belongings and desecrating their civil rights. It would produce enough cash to solve his short-term challenges and ensure he wasn't on a one-way trip back to his indigenous home, the country from which it had taken him most of his adult life to escape. The prize zone was glittering with possibility, especially as access to the crime scene was effortless, as Inderjit knew the dwelling well.

As he metaphorically rubbed his hands at the prospect of a stolen freedom, the crushing hammer of reality was leveraging into action, gathering strength to pulverise Inderjit's misaligned bubble of delusion. Inderjit knew he had not merely stepped over the line of decency, he had catapulted over it, leaving it in the far distance.

Smash! It happened.

'Did it have to be you? Why you? I trusted you. I let you into my home and this is how you repay me. Just get out!'

Every cell in Inderjit's dishonest body froze, stood still in time, in utter shock at the revelation of who lived in this house. The distressed words from the crippled Somchai vibrated through his soul and the blow of reality demolished his thoughtless, utopian world. Emotions swirled out of control as embarrassment, disgrace and degradation seeped through Inderjit's swarthy, moist skin. He had been exposed as a cruel and heartless animal, biting the hand that fed him, stealing from someone who had given him so much. The tourist had paid Inderjit handsomely to keep a watchful eye on his friend Somchai and his family. Instead he had betrayed that responsibility and wantonly torn the beating heart from the relationship. Now the potential consequences of his gross misdemeanour violently hit home.

Indignity swiftly changed to panic. The future was bleak and pointless. Inderjit's crime would most certainly result in a lengthy jail sentence in one of Thailand's notorious hell-hole prisons, a debasing ordeal that he wouldn't survive; even if he did, he would be ordered to leave the country in disgrace. There was a berserk stampede as his blood gushed to his brain. His heart sent a barrage of messages to encourage the boiling, impassioned blood.

'You can't go to prison!'

'Stop the cripple NOW! Otherwise your life is over.'

'Take this chance and clear your name, do what you need to do.'

'Think of your life, think of your family, think of their future.'

'You deserve better than prison, this was not your fault. Table six will take the blame.'

'Make a stand now or you will fall forever.'

'*Aaaaaaaaargh!*' Inderjit's war cry appeased his rabid heart. His blood filled his face, engorging his eyes with bulging animosity for the pathetic, legless mutant lying on the floor as he surged towards him and with muscle and vigour drained from deep within his stomach hit him square on the side of his head with the heavy wooden baton he was carrying for security, instantaneously breaking Somchai's scrawny neck and smashing his skull. Inderjit had grasped Somchai's life and taken it.

A warming blanket of relief enveloped Inderjit's tortured mind. His imprisonment had been evaded with bloodthirsty cruelty and had freed him from his own crime, through another monstrous crime. The momentarily creepy serenity in the murderous, blood-drenched air was disturbed by the feverish scuttling of insects which were now presented with an oozing brain and dead flesh to feast upon.

Inderjit calmly foraged through Somchai's drawers, grabbed all he could hold and ran from the crime scene, leaving a plethora of creatures from the lower end of the evolutionary scale to feed upon a being from the opposite end.

CHAPTER TWENTY NINE

The Sentence

The police investigation into Somchai's untimely demise was flippant and unconcerned. It would be one less beggar to step over in the streets, one less Bangkok inconvenience. The murder was documented and filed under 'unsolved' within hours of discovery.

Four people came to pay their final respects as the body crackled in the unforgiving flames of the funeral pyre. The orange fire glowed against Inderjit's face as his thoughts wandered back to the consequences of Somchai's death.

'For your crimes, you are now condemned to a life guilt and sorrow,' said the priest. 'You took this man's life and in return you gave yours, whoever you are, wherever you are, you will forever live in the dark shadows of regret. Somchai, be free now and fly to God's kingdom. We thank the person who freed you from this cruel existence, in return for the incarceration of their own life'

Every word the priest uttered burrowed deep into Inderjit's brain and planted a seed of penitence. With each warming thrash of the blaze the seeds began to flourish and grow into sturdy, deep-rooted trees. Inderjit stumbled home, his clothes impregnated with fumes of burning flesh and responsibility. The putrid black smoke was bellowing into the dusky sky as he looked out from his bedroom window. The trees of regretful dishonour and abasement had already blossomed into a forest of solicitude and repentance. There was no reprieve as all the light in Inderjit's life was subdued by the immense growth of regret. Branches upon branches blocked the rays of blithe spirit and superseded them with exasperation and weighty dejection. This was confinement in its most noxious form, a self-imposed denouncement, a mind in rebellious, barbed torture, unwilling to forgive or allow any compensating negations.

Every living second was a reminder of Inderjit's transgression against another human being. Somchai the saviour was now the abomination plaguing all his thoughts, a living, breathing ghost within his mind. Treacherous and unforgiving, it was the ultimate revenge. Somchai now dwelled inside Inderjit's head, coaxing and directing his moods and actions. He had earned the right to live again, to be inside his murderer, to possess a life without the burden of a physical form. Inderjit's conscience had become dutiful and binding to a life he had obliterated, taken without any shame or scruples. Now he could not function as a unique individual without the overbearing influence of a dead person.

Ironically, by the state of Thailand's law, Inderjit was granted the sole benefactor of Somchai's minuscule estate, the ultimate vengeful twist of fate. Somchai had named Inderjit as his official carer and with a mother bordering on insanity, an only child Apsara, who had recently died from a crippling disease, everything Somchai owned was bestowed upon Inderjit, except for his life's savings, which Inderjit had already callously stolen.

Inderjit was duty bound to report Somchai's demise to the English tourist who had befriended him. He wrote him a letter, knowing there was no way the tourist could ever establish the truth behind Somchai's death.

I bring you sad news. Somchai died yesterday. He had a bruise on his head but could not remember how it happened. He was very sick, so I took him to hospital, I sat with him for two hours, then he died. The doctor said Somchai had a cracked skull and internal bleeding. Somchai asked me to write to you and say thank you friend, for what you did, and he also wanted to answer your question that you asked him when you first went to his house, he just wanted you to know. He said 'everything from the day, the night, the sun to the rain. I respect I've had life, I respect that even without legs I still had life, I would die a thousand painful deaths to just live for one day. Apsara was sick but smiled every day and every smile made all my pain go away. Apsara died but her memory made me live. Whatever one suffers, as long as there is still a single breath left it's all worth it. Sleep little my friend, live and laugh very much and find yourself strong reasons that mean everything, reasons you breathe for, this will be your song, then every day you will sing your own song and you will live a life of achievement, satisfaction and passion.'

Every waking day the poignant sting of Inderjit's sentence harangued his senses. His guilt was a bleak, debilitating contamination, a malignant toxin blitzing his bloodstream, carrying its acrimony through every organ and blood cell of his body, pulsating its gruesome charge through every function. There was no deliverance, no release from his infringement of God's primordial rule, destroying another human's life, dismantling the miracle God had created. Inderjit was gradually losing the will to live with his own disappointment. His brain was possessed with an obligation to Somchai. He desperately needed redemption, to eradicate the vibration of evil he had willingly created through sheer greed and selfishness.

Through his aimless, miscreant life, Inderjit had only ever met two people who had demonstrated the uncommon essence of human kindness, pure boundless affection that was flawless, unadulterated and transparent. Benevolence that shone as truly as the rays of sunshine from the sun itself, a one-way process with nothing expected in return, ceaselessly shining with wide open arms. One of those beacons of altruism was Somchai, unfaltering in his wholeheartedness and concern for other people, even though his own world had been stripped of spirit and vitality when he had had his legs so cruelly amputated. The other humanitarian was the mysterious English tourist who had responded to Somchai and his ill-fated family with unprecedented charity. Inderjit felt a subjugate force, the first emotion since he had cold-bloodedly murdered Somchai that lifted his spirits towards humanity again. There was a deeply-burning compulsion flaring from his heart.

He knew the answer to his murderous depravity; it was the English tourist. Inderjit's liberation was in the hands of someone he had only met once. The Englishman was the closure in Inderjit's dismantled and impoverished life.

CHAPTER THIRTY

The Plague

Incessant and spasmodic movement, erratic, fevered and yet so organised. Fifty thousand bees flap their flimsy but enduring wings at a blurry, breakneck speed, thousands of times every second of every minute of every hour, every single day, until they flap themselves to death. Deep within their working home, the intensity of their noise is prolonged, chronic and ingrained, the never-ending buzz of genetic industry. Their duty, day after day after day, is to collect nectar from flowers, return to the hive, regurgitate their booty and create sturdy hexagonal honeycombs to store their secreted, gelatinous honey. They repeat this until they die.

This particular colony of bees was unique. It had one vital function of bee life missing; there was one huge difference in their otherwise inane, programmed, lifetime functioning. Just one, singular behavioural attitude separated them from the rest of the bees in existence. These bees possessed a bizarre, altered characteristic that changed the historical bee philosophy, the idiosyncrasy every bee has been born with since the beginning of the universe. These anomalous bees did not feed on the honey they were creating; they simply stored it. They had no means of sustenance, yet they survived. Their only function was to propagate a deafening fanfare of buzzing disquiet and gradually fill their homely apiary with invulnerable honeycombs and unyielding, viscous honey. Their home was as distinctive as their way of life. No hollowed tree, dark cave, dusty loft or manufactured hive was good enough for these incomparable creatures. Their custom-made dwelling was the only place where they could happily exist and compose their humming symphony and manufacture their gluey discharge. They were separated from the billions of God's other creatures that buzzed on earth, playing a vital, organic part of the complex eco-system, keeping their heavenly creative promise and playing their necessary role in the upkeep of the planet. These creatures were destructive; they only knew how to harm and destroy. A man-made cataclysm, an individual human plague, their mission was simple, far simpler than the preservation and maintenance of the environment.

They were bees of atonement. The internal melodrama of penance, the curse of regret and redress. Their immortal buzz was the disharmony and torture of an unforgivable crime. This was far greater than anything Inderjit Phal had bargained for. The metaphorical bees were getting louder and more energetic as each day passed since his heinous crime of maliciously snatching Somchai's right to live and murdering the only kindness that had ever existed in his own turbulent and rainy life. Nothing could muffle the incessant droning of guilt that had drenched Inderjit's brain and flooded his mind. The borderline between reality and hysterical dementia was severely breached as every thought, whisper and emotion that materialised in his head weighed down the balance and equation of life. His atonement bees were gradually starving his brain of rational thinking as their daily, minute by minute actions captured and dominated more and more of his sanity, clogging it with their indelible honeycomb walls.

There were only mere moments of accessibility to his own grey matter, at best for two hours of a waking day, when he could piece his thoughts together to assemble an ounce of insightful, rationale before the buzz was once again unbearable, diminishing his thinking process into the usual blurry, vexatious freefalling nightmare. Half of his brain was now irretrievable, plagued with thick, solid walls of remorse and debilitating anguish. It was just a matter of time before his self-propagating mental health would deteriorate to the unfathomable depths of alienated delusion, a corruptness of the human mind, a complete lobotomy from traditional humanity. Inderjit desperately needed to rebalance his mind. His equation had to be equalised before the burden of madness hijacked all possibility of stability and comprehension.

Another sleepless night came, with not even a chance to experience the artful bliss of five seconds of serenity, with the cruelty of a mind that doesn't catch up with reality when one first stirs from sleeping and then mercilessly catapults the victim back to the real world. Even those ruthless five seconds would have been welcome in Inderjit's fading days.

It had been six months since he had packed his troubled Bangkok life into a case and he was now in a crusty, cold city in the north of England, scraping a living from the only profession, outside of cold-blooded murder, he knew; waiting on tables. The job had been secured only through overseas Indian relatives who had paid for his fare and made him work his fingers to the bone, serving spicy food to the drunken locals in a downbeat, ramshackle restaurant.

England was the place to be. It wasn't the standard of living, the national health care or the benefit payments from the British Government that had enticed Inderjit to be treated as a slave waiter in a vile eating joint, where he was insulted, physically attacked and treated like a dog. Inderjit was after a reprieve. There was salvation in this country, which far outweighed the generosity of its welfare state. Inderjit's compulsion to find the English tourist and somehow absolve the intense burden he was carrying in his crippled mind and on his dilapidated shoulders was now his only vocation in life. It was the only balance to his grossly lopsided equation. The English tourist was the antidote to the plague that was gratuitously, cannibalising his life. Thoughts of tracking down and meeting the tourist were the only sane thinking which calmed the atonement bees, and yet it was also their steroid elixir to grow stronger and more disruptive. The vicious circle whirlwinding round and round in Inderjit's head was never-ending. Was the inhumane buzzing the onset of madness, leading to thoughts of tracking down the tourist? Or was the absurd obsession with the tourist and confessing to murder bending his mind? Either way, the conglomerated mess rampaging through his senses was warped into one singular sensation, a riot of emotions that possessed no conclusion or reasoning.

Hundreds and hundreds of times Inderjit had played the scene in his tortured mind, of how he would approach the tourist, what he would say, the words he would use, and most importantly, how he would feel once he had told the tourist the bitter, twisted truth.

As each day passed the perpetual fracas in his head became more and more oppressive. The infernal racket was bursting from his ears and deafening the reality of the world. Inch by inch his sanity was being conquered, overcome by a psychotic momentum that was potentially dangerous to himself and anyone that was involved in his convoluted circle of maniacal reflections. The murder of Somchai had lost its criminality and subsequently been downgraded to a nonchalant happening, almost normal, and even worse, borne of obligation.

Delirious Cake

The cornerstone of great cake baking – follow the instructions and the result will emulate the delightful pictures in the cookbook and taste as good as the description. The base constituent of all cakes is flour, finely ground from cereal grains, milled to delicate chalky perfection, patiently waiting in a bowl for all its fellow additives before the heat of the oven expands the soggy mixture and causes its proud uprising. Precise quantities, specific ingredients, vigorous mixing, the correct temperature, and the result will tantalise the taste buds.

The delirious cake worked in a less appetising way. This was the deadly metaphor of mental deterioration in Inderjit's head. Every thought, sensation and emotion was added to the mixture, which was zealously stirred on a daily basis until it was an unrecognisable, bitter mass of suffering and isolation. It was a burdensome cake crammed with delectable ingredients but in grossly unbalanced measures, creating a volatile concoction, heated by the perpetual buzzing plague of bees. Inderjit's mental uprising had begun. The homicidal amalgam was scorching with anguish and a compulsion to exonerate itself from the delirious parody that had expanded into every ounce of his conscience. It was now time to remove the grotesque mixture from the overheated oven and present it to the world.

CHAPTERTHIRTYTWO

Deliverance

An entangled mesh of oppression, contorted, criss-crossing, overlapping and knotted in complexity. We are innocently born into freedom and violently terrorised into servitude, enslaved by life itself. There is no deliverance, no pity and no liberation from the burden of living with only one single assurance available. The only declaration that is a guaranteed pledge. The unrivalled equation of balance in the equation of life. Death. Patiently waiting to deliver us from our malignant and exploited days of perseverance. We are all born with a signed death warrant, the only credential we can whole heartedly rely on to grant its macabre promise. A certificate that is undated but tenacious and non-negotiable.

Michael was silently standing in line. It was pitch black, and the sack tied around his head was eliminating all the light and exposure to the world. All his senses were embroiled in a sinister plot, conjuring stories and images of vileness, desperation and death. Otherwise alert human senses were confused and in their confusion their inbred optimism was overshadowed by the darkness of the unknown.

Swoooooosh! Ching! Thud!

The chilling combination of noises brought vomit from deep within his churned stomach. It was the terrifying sounds of execution as a razor-sharp guillotine glided down the rickety wooden frame and effortlessly sliced off the head of whoever had been forced to kneel below and place their neck on the curved positioning block. The decapitated head, with its horrified frozen expression, in the midst of its final breath, dropped into the waiting wicker basket.

Michael felt a tight grip around his arm as he was shuffled and coerced into the position of instant death. It was his turn, as he was forcefully pushed face down onto the wooden block, feeling his own sour sick, cold and clinging to his sweating face. Death was inevitable as the countdown to his demise began. Emotion electrified his shaking body and trembled his innards with fear. The executor gladly tugged the rope operating the ghastly mechanism designed with only one purpose in mind, swift murder, and the steel blade was set free to carry out its only job. It descended at breakneck speed and cut Michael's life short.

Michael gave a hysterical convulsion and with a jerking shiver he gratefully woke from the nightmare. Five seconds of delight following the realisation that it was all a dream, and Michael's bona fide nightmare was initiated as reality became more surreal and lurid than being a victim of execution by guillotine.

'My life has turned to dust and you are the evil volcano that forced me from the earth, interrupted my joyful existence and melted my future into nothingness. Your English blood money turned me into a murderer. Your blood money forced me to kill Somchai. No, you killed Somchai, it was your blood money that killed Somchai. You are the murderer. You and your money have ruined my life. God wants his revenge and I must grant God's wish, or he will send me to hell. But you cannot escape the wrath of the Almighty, you too must pay your debt. You too have to suffer. I will liberate you from this earth, otherwise you too will be hell bound.

I am your liberator, I will free you from this loathsome world. I will release your burdens and you will come to heaven with me, where we will both be free men and we can meet our old friend Somchai, who is patiently waiting for us. Imagine his face when we turn up. Imagine how pleased he will be that we both found heaven!'

An introduction was not necessary; Michael had established who the intruder in his bedroom was. Inderjit had found him. He had found the English tourist and seeing the brass ornament on the floor, which was usually on his bedside table, he knew it had been used to bludgeon him unconscious. Inderjit had knocked him out with Rodin's 'The Kiss' while he was asleep. The beautiful gift sent to him from the bottom of Rebecca's heart had been turned into a deadly weapon. That also explained the searing pain in his head.

Michael was unable to respond to Inderjit's incoherent rambling. His mouth was taped shut and his body incapacitated, tightly tied to his bedroom chair. Michael was helpless, at the hands of a waiter he had befriended in Bangkok who had just admitted to the murder of Somchai. None of this situation made any sense. Was it just another nightmare? Was this really happening? Was this really the hapless, illiterate but trustworthy Inderjit?

'Look at me when I talk to you. You will thank me when we reach heaven, my friend. You will thank me over and over again for releasing you from this prison we are both condemned to, unless we are freed of the mountainous guilt that is weighing our lives into the ground. The guilt of destroying an innocent life, of leaving a family to die without their only provider, the guilt of taking the life of a feeble, helpless cripple - we did that, you were the evil puppet master and I was the innocent puppet who operated when you pulled the strings. Why did you pick me? Why did you make me your puppet? Why did you steal my life? Why? Why? Why? Why? Why? What did I ever do to deserve this pain? The noise in my head never stops. Do you know why there is noise in my head? I know why. This noise that haunts me night and day is the pain Somchai felt when I beat his head senseless, it's what he felt in his brain as I took his life with one heavy blow. Now that pain is all mine, while Somchai rests in peace. I'm suffering day and night with the same hurt over and over and over again. Do you know what this noise feels like? Do you? Do you? Do you Michael? No, you don't, you don't know what pain is. You don't know what suffering is. You don't know how Somchai suffered. You don't understand pain. Do you?'

The Kiss

'The Kiss', a sculpture created in 1889 by Auguste Rodin. It depicts Francesca da Rimini, a 13th century noblewoman who fell in love with her husband's younger brother Paolo, who was also married. The couple were discovered and killed by Francesca's husband. The lovers' lips do not actually touch in the sculpture, suggesting they were interrupted and met their demise without partaking in a kiss. A tragic, tortured love affair. Rapture and pathos, an idiosyncratic companionship depicting the kiss that could seal the betrothal of love and passion and yet ill-fated, merely seconds from slaughter. An enchanted devotion, seductive passionate love, warped and shrouded with pessimistic bleakness, idolised in a beautiful, misunderstood sculpture. Everlasting, romantic love or doomed, star-crossed lovers? Did their pending dissolution from life consummate the love affair or did it crudely hinder and abort all the promises they had cemented their adulterous relationship with? A paradox of love, a twist in fate, a cruel treachery. The enigma of lovers, now arduously transformed into a lethal weapon brandished by a psychopath with a farcical vendetta.

'Let me show you. Mr Michael. Let me show you what the noise feels like. When you can feel my pain, you will understand the importance of releasing ourselves from this prison of death we have become captive in. This noise buzzes in my head every day and every night, it feeds on my brain, it is slowly dissolving my life until there will be nothing. You will feel the same noise, then we can escape together, we can escape the noise.'

In the first volume of *Divine Comedy* an epic poem penned in 1308 by Dante Alighieri describing his travels through hell, purgatory and heaven, Dante meets Francesca da Rimini and her lover Paola in the second circle of hell, reserved for the lustful. In this damned abyss, the couple are trapped in an eternal whirlwind doomed to be forever swept through the air just as they allowed themselves to be swept away by their passions. Dante faints after calling out to Francesca and hearing the details of her plight, abandoned for an eternity to wallow in the quagmire of their despicable sins.

There was total darkness. The brass lovers, murdered by the hostile, estranged husband, delivered a skull-crunching knockout to Michael's already injured head. Michael was caught in the whirlwind as his hammered mind circled and frantically spun out of control and tumbled into lurid bewilderment. Dante was not present to hear his ordeal; there was nothing except grim bleakness.

'Where are you my Angel? Where are you? Please come to me, I need you. I need you my Angel. Where are you?'

The cold, damp mist falling onto Michael's face was his only company in the opaque, abandoned space, an expanse with no dimensions and no closure. It was too dark to see anything, but Michael knew it wasn't just the lack of light restricting his vision. His blindness had returned. He had entered his own circle of perdition, an unearthly personal hell. A deep sensibility within his tortured mind told him his entire life was on display, his movie reel was playing. It was sheer nakedness. He was vulnerable and exposed and yet there was no one watching and his own eyes were incapable of viewing the bizarre context of transgressions and virtues that had littered his days, but his sensitised ears could hear familiar noises approaching, a buzzing cacophony of shrill sounds, voices in unison directed at him. Something had been uprooted, almost revived at his arrival. There was a sense of depraved vibration in the air, resonating anxiety into every distressed ounce of his body. Was this death? Was he now dead? Expelled from his human form, blind in the afterlife, compounded by the burden of dread and fear of the unknown.

'You've come home, we've been waiting for you. It's been too long.'

Vision was not necessary. Every minuscule detail became visual. Michael's blindness merely exacerbated the spectacularly disturbing reality. He couldn't see who the collective voices belonged to, yet the prolific images in his imagination, painted a macabre sight.

There was a cloud of choking grey dust, fine particles reminiscent of dusty chalk boards and teachers endlessly scrawling their teachings onto them. The penetrating screech of the chalk inscribing the black slate was now instilled into the harshness of voices bellowing from the three underworld creatures that had floated into Michael's desolation. Their clothes were torn to shreds and decaying on the crumbling limbs that only rotting death manifests. The chalk dust was years of putrefied skin separating from their decomposing bodies, displaying eroding skeletons. The grey, disintegrating bones were etched with the decades of miserable pain and torture of the life they had once sustained, a pain that was embodied in the evilness of their deep-set, bloodied eyeballs. The monstrosities epitomised illness, affliction and the deterioration of fallen souls, mental asphyxiation and the suffering of crucifixion.

'We've come to take you away, your life is ours now. You are dead. We will take you to eternal death. We will take you to pain. We will make you suffer. We will torture your soul every day and every night, forever and ever.'

Each screeching word that bellowed from their festering faces pierced Michael's body with a deep wound, lacerating his skin with doom and fear. This was hell. The very anticipation of a condemned life was hell itself. The creatures floated closer, stretching out their skeletal arms to force Michael into the bottomless pit of abuse and agony.

'No, no, no, no, no you don't exist, you can't exist! I created you. I made you. You were always in my mind, you didn't really exist. You cannot be real. You are witches from my imagination. You do not exist. You do not exist. You do not exist. You do not exist!'

Thwack! Inderjit slapped Michael back to reality. Startled and bleeding from the violent encounter with Francesca and Paolo, Michael returned from his personal bewitched hell to another depth of hell. Reality.

'I do exist. I am here and I will take you away from all this pain. Can you hear the noise now? Is it now inside your head? Are we now both together? We need to be free my friend. We need to travel to a land where we will be reunited and live our lives free of burden, guilt and regret. Don't cry. Don't struggle. Once we have burned our lives free of this earth, the pain in your head will disappear and we can live in the beauty of heaven and meet our old friend.'

Michael's eyes were stinging, uncontrollably weeping. He was too frightened for any other emotion. It was a caustic, biting pain and there was something in his eyes, affecting his vision, something his body was attempting to cleanse with a waterfall of crying. The smell in the air created a level of personal hell that Dante had never envisaged throughout his glorious descriptions and travels through purgatory.

The smell was petrol. Michael was doused in it; entirely drenched to his shaking bones as the flammable vapours distorted the sullen air.

'We need deliverance from our sins. We need deliverance from this sinful world. We will not have deliverance until we feel the suffering Somchai's soul felt as he was burnt to ashes. If we can deliver ourselves from evil, in the same way Somchai was relieved of his body, then we will go to heaven. The price we will pay today will be rewarded tenfold when we discharge this life and liberate our soul into the hands of God.'

Inderjit lifted the container, which had been out of Michael's restricted view, and poured the contents upon himself.

'It's cold, but don't worry my friend it will soon heat up and take us to God, where we will be warm forever,' he said.

Death is silence. Death is darkness. Death is closure. In isolation silence, darkness and closure can be the consequences of a multitude of situations and not necessarily unwanted repercussions. All three are desirable throughout life, and in many circumstances absolutely essential. The severity of death and the unknown void that may exist is derided by the anticipation of forthcoming death. The sheer earthquake of human misery in the dying moments of the grand spectacle of life that is uniquely granted, whether by celestial forces or by natural, cosmic evolution is greater than death itself.

The cloaked master of destruction glides into view, his shadowy skull creaks into a skeletal grin, encompassing all that is feared and misunderstood throughout life. Every moment of ignorant ingratitude for the blessed breath of consciousness is now clasped within his relentless, bony grip. Suffering, torment and mortification are not death. Death is a mere comforting pillow that soothes the violation and rape of one's soul as death becomes the destination. The road to oblivion, death's highway, is uniquely both the shortest and longest journey ever undertaken, and the driving seat in the vehicle of doom is occupied by the being that awaits all your living days from the opening of your Mother's womb to the penultimate moments of your hallowed life, the reaper himself. Death is too beautiful, too glorious, too prodigious, to simply wash over your life. The blackness of dying becomes the rainbow of ultimate artistry, once feared but now respected and revered as the ultimate prize of life itself.

An interview with Death

'Today is the day I've been waiting for. Today we have an exceptional treat for you lucky viewers. Our special guest today, is the one and only Mr Death himself, and I'll be asking him all those things you've always wanted to know about the dark destroyer, all those questions you were always afraid to ask. So let's waste no more time, because we all know how short life is and how we're running out of time. Ladies and gentlemen, please welcome DEATH himself!

'Hello Death, it's great to have you on the show. You're clearly a very busy man, with so many lives to take. Talking of which, tell me when I'm going to die, c'mon Mr Death, when are you coming to get me? Hopefully it's not before the end of the show!'

'Thank you, it's great to be here, I've been waiting for the invite. Not an invite to the show but an invite to come for your soul.'

'Ha, ha, ha, Mr Death has a sense of humour. So when's my time up? Hit me with the truth, Mr Death. I'm not scared. It's only death, who cares? When your time is up, it's up, so when are you coming for me? This week, this month, this year? Will I get to see my fiftieth birthday? C'mon Mr Death, I need to know and I'm sure the viewers want to know so they no longer have to watch me on television.'

'I really don't know. That's the truth. Let me explain. When humans are blessed with the gift of life I get a message advising me of the new birth. Then nothing. Nothing happens until you're ready to leave this earth. That's when I get a second message, and that is when I come and pay you a visit.'

'So let me understand what you're saying, Mr Death. You don't cause death, you don't pursue it. You only arrive on the scene when you get a message telling you we're about to die. So Mr Death, please excuse my naivety, but you're no more than a glorified undertaker. In fact let me take this a step further, you're not even that, we have plenty of undertakers already, you seem to have no purpose other than being a mythical being that simply scares the shit out of people. We don't really need you, do we Mr Death? You really have no reason to exist, do you? You're a fraud, Mr Death!'

'You poor confused, deluded mortal! You are naïve indeed. An undertaker? Please don't insult me, I don't make a profit from death as they do. I only profit in your doom. My untold riches come from human misery, from your pain, from your regret, but they are not financial rewards, my reward is far more satisfying than money could ever be. You cannot possibly understand my role in your demise until I get the message to pay you a visit. Then you will fully comprehend my importance. I'm looking forward to meeting you on your judgement day. Then you will acknowledge what I do and the monumental relevance of my presence.'

'Mr Death, I'm sorry but you don't scare me. You're a fake. You have fooled and belittled people for an eternity. It really is time you came clean. It's time for you to admit, you're no more than a circus clown, created in medieval times, probably to scare little children. You have deceived and corrupted the minds of innocent people. If you were human you'd be serving a very long sentence behind bars for your heinous crimes against humanity. Mr Death, you're an antiquated con artist who needs to admit to the world right now, on live television, that your existence is a sham, a huge mockery feeding on the fears of mankind. Over to you. The time has come to remove your hood, take off your cloak and retire. We don't want you. We hate you. Be gone, Death!'

'You're right, you don't want me and I know you hate me, after all I am Death itself. I am the unknown. I am the darkness. I am beyond this world. I am the black void of nothingness. I am fear itself, resonating in every ounce of your blood, impregnating it with anguish and dread. I am eternal and I will visit everyone on this earth, I will visit all of you and then I will visit the yet unborn, the children of your children's children. They will all know my name. They will all fear me. They will all fear their destiny. Death is here to stay. Every one of you was born to die. Every one of you belongs to me.'

'Well Mr Death, I think you're proving yourself to be more stupid than I ever thought you were. I gave you this one opportunity, while the world was watching, to do the dignified thing, to have an ounce of integrity and simply admit to the good people of this planet that you're no more than a bleak, archaic fairy-tale that doesn't have any belonging in the modern world. But instead you've maintained your pathetic arrogance, and furthermore you've attempted to heighten your contemptible parody. Death, you are a disgrace. However, I'm a good-natured human being and I'm going to give you one final opportunity to tell the world you're no more than a dishonourable blemish, deliberately plaguing the inhabitants of this immaculate sphere.'

'You belligerent imbecile! You have left me with no option but to prove my existence. You will live to regret that you ever tested my supremacy.'

'Is that a threat, Mr Death? You don't scare me. Go on then.

Prove yourself. Tell us what you do, almighty one. We're all listening with bated breath. I warn you now, the world is watching and it wants answers. You can no longer be the oppressor of humankind. This is your one and only chance.'

'I say it once again. You will live to regret your wretched pettiness for questioning your own fate. When I get the calling to relieve you of your paltry existence I will take you on a pilgrimage of your life. Your final vision will be the misdeeds you've done and the immense burden of penitence that will make your departure a welcome retreat.'

'C'mon, c'mon, c'mon give it to me, let's go on my journey. You know as well as I do, Mr Death, I have no regrets in this life. The only regret I have today is inviting a pointless has-been such as you onto my show. You are nothing short of a disgrace!'

'SILENCE! You insignificant puppet! Your regrets will weigh upon your soul and corrode the lives of many people who you have violated and destroyed through your arrogance and depravity. People will celebrate your death, and the indelible scars you have endowed society with will become your epitaph. You have coerced me to show the world your evil life. So be it!'

'I'm waiting, Mr Death. I've done nothing the world will ever disagree with. Your woeful pantomime doesn't fool anyone, and I want an immediate apology for what you've just insinuated. You are pathetic. You don't scare me!'

'There will be no apologies. The world will finally see behind your mask of foul deceit, and then the one thing you have violated will end, your heinous life will be no more, as you will remember the terrible things you have conveniently forgotten. The world will hate you with a remorseless passion as it blesses your demise.'

'Mr Death, you are the one in violation. I haven't forgotten a thing, my life is clean and innocent. I think it's time for you to leave the show. You are a loathsome and disgusting monster that needs to disappear for good. Goodbye Mr Death, and good riddance'

'Silence, you fool! How could you forget you're a soulless murderer? The distressed parents of Louise Miller need to know the truth, the truth of how she will never return home to her loving family. The truth about how she lies silently rotting in the grounds of your very own dwelling, her final experience on this earth being the blinding pain of cigarette burns as you laughingly stubbed them into her innocent sixteen-year-old eyes and inhaled the smoke as her tears extinguished the flame. How could you forget her begging you for mercy as you relentlessly raped and humiliated her? How could you forget her screams of torment as you sliced her skin from her beaten body and urinated on the bleeding wounds, all to amuse your depravity and disrespect for human life? Your depravity and disrespect has no limits. It could only be satisfied by the knowledge that you buried her alive, watching her choke on the soil filling her mouth and clouding her eyes as they cried blood. Now my friend, your life is over. Within twenty-four hours you will beg me for mercy. I bid you farewell and I look forward to our inescapable reunion, when I will remind you of all your other abominable crimes against the life you were blessed with. Goodbye for now, little man!'

The Kiss Of Death

'I'm ready. I'm coming to find you. Forgive me mother, forgive me father, this is my destiny. I didn't want to come into this world, you brought me here against my will. I will now return and complete the journey. My friend awaits me. I must go. Fire, take me home!'

There was intense hunger, an unsatisfied urge that was desperate for fulfilment, an eternal thirst longing for a quenching absolution as the single spark from the match Inderjit struck against the matchbox sprang into omnipotent splendour. The dream was alive. Inderjit's matchstick was never destined to simply light candles or the tips of cigarettes serving the futile whims of mere humans, to then be shaken or blown into insignificance, drained of the potential it was born for. This match was on the brink of unmitigated glory as its colleagues watched, in awe of the brilliance about to commence. The spark sucked in the combustible petrol fumes solemnly searching for a master to serve and immediately its minute structure transformed into an uncompromising leopard with pure sinewy muscles and fangs of carnage and elimination. It was conscious and groomed to gorge on everything in its path. Miraculous encounters like these were rare and not to be understated in this opportunity of a lifetime. The spark ruthlessly grabbed at every powerhouse petrol droplet and multiplied with unstoppable arrogance in an attempt to satisfy its timeless starvation to burn and devour.

'Somchai! Somchai! Somchai! Somchai!'

After four pained, screeching gasps of Somchai's name, Inderjit was unable to produce any more sounds from his burning face. His lips, nose and eyes amalgamated in the furnace and disintegrated. Inderjit's eyeballs popped and squirted out their gelatinous content in a futile attempt to slow the blinding rage of the fire. The communication to his conscience ceased. The scale of pain thresholds had been violated and there was little purpose in reminding his body that there was danger to be avoided. With complete shutdown seconds away, his final thought pattern struggled to cascade through Inderjit's melting mind. With that thought and eyes incapable of vision, a mouth almost disintegrated down to the bone of his jawline and with teeth peering out from his smouldering gums, he lunged forward towards Michael and collapsed onto his strapped lap, embracing him with his burning limbs and pressed his annihilated, burning face upon Michael's face.

'I love you, I love you, I love you, I love you, I love you, I love you!'

The Kiss was transformed into a modern-day work of flaming, murderous art as Inderjit burned onto Michael's body in almost the precise pose the medieval lovers had been caught in. Francesca da Rimini and her lover Paola watched in admiration as the two men plagiarised Rodin's classic sculpture in a blaze of ravenous fire. Fiercer than a plague of famished locusts, the fire leapt onto Michael in an attempt to dissolve the two humans into one mass of burning flesh, hair and bones glued together by the cataclysmic heat. The ferocity of the vision made the second level of hell appear like a welcome retreat as Inderjit's bodily organs exploded, splattering boiling blood into the flames.

Michael's exasperated final pangs of breath surged from his cauterised lungs. Numb to the unforgiving agony, a darkness appeared in his subconscious mind. There were no words required, no expressions or explanations necessary. Death had arrived, and Michael's journey was about to commence. The concluding chapter was a ride through life's defining moments, with the grim reaper as the concierge of bereavement.

CHAPTER THIRTYSIX

The Pilgrimage

'Wake up, wake up, wake up, wake up, please wake up, please, please wake up!'

Michael's father was a calm, collected man, not usually perturbed by any adversity, but now he was presented with a teenage son he couldn't revive. The boy's his limbs trembled and his heartbeat poured a lava of disconcerted emotion from his otherwise stern, unfazed composure. Young Michael wasn't moving. There was a blanched, clammy look on his face, an expression that didn't flinch as his father's frantic tears dripped onto his pallid skin. Michael, this young child, was clearly wandering the corridor of life searching for an exit door to leave earth behind.

A red hot branding iron was melting through his father's chest, glowing with fire, indelibly searing his skin. Tunnelling into his beating heart, I was wittingly destroying the soft sentimental tissue and swiftly burning ingrained carnage coupled with an all-consuming pain, an erasable memory of protracted suffering. A parent's worst fear was a becoming a harsh reality as a child was disappearing from the life they had miraculously created. A baby that once had the words 'I love you with all my heart and I will do all I can to keep you safe' whispered into its new born ears was departing the life he had been blessed with. A life that had brought such happiness, such unadulterated beauty and such unconditional love, was now being snatched from existence, whisked away into the unknown darkness of death.

'Michael, Michael, Michael, you can't die, you can't leave us. Please help God, please!'

The inaugural scene of Michael's pilgrimage was utter devastation, as he watched the excruciating torture he had deliberately dragged his parents through. Mr Death's chaperone duty had surpassed his own job description as the pain of Mum and Dad watching their son give up on life was tearing Michael's soul apart. Every ounce of distressed emotion he had contrived upon his innocent parents was multiplied a thousand times with the relentless bite of regret and self-disgust. Every tear he witnessed was a bloody bite of his flesh, a mouthful of his apologetic, penitent skin and fibres. He was naked in a tank of hungry, carnivorous piranha fish and they were whittling his woeful body down to its heartsick bones, callously devouring him bite by bite.

'But I survived, I didn't die. The paramedics arrived in time to save my life. I know Mum and Dad were happy afterwards, I know they didn't suffer for long, I know the hurt didn't last. I didn't mean to take so many sleeping tablets, I was just curious, that's all. Nothing but curious. I was a curious child, a stupid, thoughtless curious child who just wanted to see what would happen with a mouthful of sleeping tablets.'

The unstoppable piranhas of bitter regret were impervious to Michael's protestations. Mr Death's intention was torment, grief and misery, not an opportunity to bargain for leniency. Their barbarous teeth unmercifully continued the deserved butchery of Michael's body.

'Ok, I'm sorry, I'm sorry. What more do you want from me? I'm sorry Mum, I'm sorry Dad, I didn't mean to hurt you, I'm so sorry, I can't stand this pain any more, just take me away and let me die in peace. Please, I'm already dead. Please let me go. I'm sorry!'

CHAPTER THIRTYSEVEN

Wretched Life

The rigid *'thud, thud, thud, thud'* dampened by the irreverent clouds of lardy, impenetrable fat, a consequence of obesity, was begging to stop. It was getting harder and harder for Michael's mother's heart to carry on the programmed sequence of pumping blood around the body. Once upon a time it had been so easy, such an unequivocal, straightforward task, but decades of poor health and diet had fought wars with the heart on the battleground of the expanding body mass, and each onslaught had left its disabling smudge in the operation of the crimson pump. The heart wasn't one for defeat. It soldiered on amidst the barbaric penetration and battering of killer carbohydrates, metamorphosing fats and malignant drugs that were shrewdly disguised as essential medicines.

'I can't do it any more, doctor. It just won't shift, I've taken all the tablets, I've done all I can. It hurts me every single waking day. I can't sleep and throughout my days all I want to do is hide and disappear from the world. I want to die. If I can't lose my weight, I don't want to live.'

The doctor's lacklustre expression was as starched and listless as his white lab coat. There was no excuse he hadn't been tearfully told before, no bleat from a carelessly porcine world he hadn't heard, no merciful request for slimming tablets he hadn't been besieged with. Just another irresponsible person, from a gorging, heedless world where eyes and greed were proportionately larger than the need for extra calories. To an observer the diabolical self-inflicted rotundness was a laughing matter and the cornerstone of hysterical jokes, in a society where largeness was viewed with circus-freak entertainment rather than a disease that would one day become an epidemic throughout the western world, but to Michael it was another injection of blight rushing through his inanimate veins. The sight of his mum desperately overweight and helpless, unable to sleep or lead a life of normality, pleading for medical assistance from a scathing doctor was another bullet of shameful blame.

'Mum, I know you can't hear me, I know it's just too late, I know I shouldn't have stolen your slimming medicine but I was fat and I hated myself. I'd hate myself for a hundred years if I'd known what I did to you. It was the boys at school, they said I was fat, they called me names. I didn't deserve that, I didn't deserve any of that. It wasn't my fault I stole your medicine. It was the boys at school, it was all their fault. All their fault that I hurt you so much. All their fault that I took your pills and replaced the contents with sugar. I didn't mean to poison you with sugar. I desperately needed to be thin. I'm so sorry but I'm not to blame, I needed your pills but I'm sorry I hurt you so much.'

Playground taunts of 'you're really fat' had started Michael's irreversible mudslide of taking medicine prescribed for adults. Three simple words were a cyclone of despair circling round and round Michael's pre-teen mind. Harmless playground banter from unkind children was enough to stave away vital sleep and effect Michael's day-time functioning and more importantly his self-esteem. Obesity was not a challenge, however three words in a fatal expression into an impressionable mind were enough to exaggerate a self-image into the girth and weight of a mountain when looking into a mirror and steal Mum's dieting and sleeping medication.

There was an abrupt change in temperature, from an unnoticeable placid climate to a bitterly cold wind that shivered Michael's burning bones even in the afterlife. The doctor's grimace froze as he stared at his clipboard, which detailed Mum's gradual demise in health and burgeoning increase in circumference. With an almost fluid swerve on the doctor's couch, Mum was standing up, and with her anciently pained eyes staring directly into Michael, suddenly she was there, the surgery was a theatrical backdrop, she had left the distressed past and supernaturally transcended into Michael's pilgrimage of darkness.

'You pathetic little boy. How dare you! How dare you visit the misdeeds of your wretched life and blame others for the damage you caused. All the heartbreak is your fault. Every tear was caused by you. Your evil wrongdoings cursed the family and the curse killed us a hundred times over. Now be gone, leave us in peace and live your eternal grave with the regret and torture you deserve.'

With a bitter quake benumbing Michael's conscience, there was little to be misunderstood. Death's migration through life was a reminding reprimand, a lifetime of debacle and self-reproach, a final chance to apologise for the infernal deeds that caused pain and sorrow. A personal anthology of remorseful hell.

One final prayer

'Four thousand pounds and I will rid you of the evil stalking your son. If you can't pay then I can't solve your problem, and it is a serious problem, one that will shortly lead to his death. It's up to you. You either find the money or you son dies. He's had a lucky escape so far because the paramedics arrived on time. The spell is gradually devouring him, he won't be so lucky next time'

The piercing torture that gushed with each word spouted from the soothsayer's mouth bellowed through Michael as he felt the bludgeoned hearts of his troubled parents sink with the dreaded news.

'There's no value in crying, so dry your tears. You either find the cash or your son will be no more. That's the problem with witchcraft. It gets hold of you and doesn't stop biting until your worldly flesh is no more. Someone evil has cast that spell upon him, and it is your duty as parents to save him from his painful fate. I'm giving you a discount. Four thousand pounds is nothing compared to the danger I will put myself in to free your son from the devil's work and nothing when it comes to saving his innocent life, a life that you brought into this world. A twisted world that is now so eager to take him back.'

An ocean of shame washed over Michael. He gasped for air,

left breathless as the water of deceit filled his lungs that once breathed such easy lies.

'Mum, Dad don't listen to him, please don't give him any money! There were no witches, no evil eyes staring at me, no creatures sitting on my bed and no terrible nightmares. I just wanted attention. I just wanted to be noticed. I was resentful and scarred by the taunts at school. I just wanted to feel special. There were no monsters after me. It was just stories I'd overheard you talking about, stories that I made my own, to cover up for the sudden illness caused by the sleeping pills. The only monster in your life was me. The overdose of sleeping pills wasn't witchcraft, it was my evilness, my stupid, stupid, selfishness. I'm so sorry!'

Tears of stress and sorrow channelled through the creases of depression, meandering down their faces as they handed over a wad of crumpled banknotes.

'It's all the money we have. We've sold all we could sell. Please take it and do your best to free our son from the beast within him. Do whatever you need to do and send the black magic spell back to the one that besmirched our lives with it. We have a second chance with him, we already lost him once. We cannot let that happen again.'

A pang of fear and distress harpooned Michael as his parents, dispirited and forlorn faded into a blurry haze of melancholy, setting the scene for his ongoing, never ending sojourn through the gloom of his villainy.

Echoes reverberating through time and space reacted positively with the dampened human psyche. Powerfully stirring the soul, manipulating an uplifting aura, a renewed confidence. A sincere belief that as a last opportunity, there is still that glowing beacon of hope that will guide us through the murk. Somewhere above those silent, hand-joined wishes and desires are met with the celestial magic of godliness. Faith comes to all when the need is severe enough and the solution is unfathomable.

'Dearest God, I have forever been your servant and never have I complained when you've forced me to walk on broken glass. With bleeding feet I have left injured, bloody footprints to your door and worshipped you endlessly. Are you there? Are you there when we need you? Will you carry us through our tortured lives? Will you please remove the burden that you have tested our lives with? We can't survive any more darkness. The weight is now unbearable and we are dying a slow, wounding death. You've sent us demons that taunt us with their sorcery, you've sent us soothsayers that have stolen our money, you've sent us all the grief any human can handle and still our son is unwell. If you are there, then release us from this grip of ongoing evil and deliver us to the happiness we've never asked of you before. Please let Surine Devata be the answer we seek. Every ounce of income you've blessed our lives with is now gone, we are destitute, we have lost all our worldly possessions to pay for the path you've shown us. I will never ask anything else of your almighty being. One final prayer that Surine will bring us salvation, deliver us from pain and give us back our son. Amen.'

Dad's tearful prayer fired another sharp bullet of incorrigible pain through Michael's broken resolve. Simple little selfish mistakes had brought the people dearest to his life to their knees in despair. Hell really was darkness and harassment beyond any human measure. The bellowing fires of the underworld may cause unbounded suffering but were no more than a welcome spark compared to the wrenched heartstrings of irreparably dismembered emotions.

'Dad, Dad, Dad, please hear me, please don't cry! I'm dead now, but this is worse than death. The pain I rained upon you is death in itself. I didn't want to do that, I didn't want you to suffer. I didn't want you to cry. I didn't want anything except your happiness. I know I'm damned and I deserve to suffer and for an eternity I will remember the sadness and trouble I rained upon your poor lives.'

The coldness returned, and with it came a gaunt stillness, frozen in a timeless entity, shrouded by the misery of lamenting penance as Dad's kneeling mumblings to God abruptly stopped. His head turned and directed a vexed stare at Michael. Without movement, Michael's breathing stopped and hot gushes of blood filled his face. His eyes bulged with fright. Dad was in his face, his pallid weeping skin and eyes fuelled with violence and anger, almost amalgamated into Michael's being. Dad's bony, wrinkled hands were wrapped around Michael's neck, shaking him uncontrollably as his windpipe crunched and restricted the movement of air. There was a tarry blackness in Dad's mouth as the monstrous decaying figure, once his beloved, devoted father, began to devour his face. It appeared to open wider than Michael's head as poisonous words wrapped in a cold fog poured from him, each word melting upon Michael's already dead features like sulphurous acid.

'You have consumed us! You have killed us! You have sent us to hell. You deserve death. You are death! Go and suffer! You are suffering, you are pain. You are hell. Be gone, be gone and never return!'

Every word was a doomed cloud of despair and darkness as pitch blackness spewed over Michael. Even in death there was pain, an intensity that could not be suffered in life. Death was not an escape, merely an accursed beginning.

CHAPTER THIRTY NINE

Revenge

'He came into my life and stole every sacred breath I had been blessed with and kidnapped my soul. It wasn't time for me to go, but I had no choice. I am now roaming with the undead, living my personal hell. I'm not alive, because he took my mind, I'm not dead, because death never came to me. I went to death. Now my flowers are dead. They will never bloom and my life is doomed to be a desperate hole of nothingness with a legacy of hatred left behind me. Why did he do this to me? Why did he choose me? Why did he choose me to die and live forever in the evil wake of my own living death?'

Michael reluctantly watched as Rosie scrawled the bright scarlet words into her diary. Her writing instrument was an orange knife, and the ink was blood flowing from a gaping wound in her chest. As she dipped the blade into the cut, seeping redness gushed over her hand. The tip of sharpness poked at the torn membrane of her heart as it scratched past her jagged, broken ribcage. Michael was speechless, knowing any noise from his mouth would aggravate Rosie and he would have to bear her angst for causing the anguish and misery he had bestowed upon her.

A stark, prickly realisation dawned upon him as Rosie's demise filtered into his brain. The trail of happenings from his consultation as a child to her tortured mind and subsequently her dreadful suicide was entirely his fault. Fabricated stories of witches and demons from a harmless, insecure and imaginative mind had cursed her final years as the guilt of such a charmed and amicable woman dying a horrendous death added another weight of remorse around Michael's already heavily-laden neck.

'My darling Rick. I miss you so. I miss you so much. My evil murderer is here. He is watching me. He is watching me suffer as I live the lifeless life he forced me into. Take your revenge, Rick! Come and get him! Come and take him away. He killed us. He stole our lives. He broke our minds. Come on my darling, you've been waiting for this moment. Come and free us from this evil man that took so much from us, come and pay him back for our tortured love.'

Her eyes were withdrawn into their sockets and circled in rooted black lines from hundreds of sleepless nights as she suddenly looked up and scowled, grinding her teeth in anger. There was another presence in the room, behind Michael. It was another person. In a flash there was a thick noose over Michael's head and almost simultaneously it was forced down and tightened around his neck. Michael's breathing stopped, but his eyes remained wide open to witness every minute detail of the spectacle, as Rosie leapt over her desk and flew into his body, wielding the blood-dipped orange knife. She plunged it deeply into his heart with a force that would have knocked him over had it not been for Rick standing behind him with the tourniquet squeezed around his neck.

'Take that, you evil bastard! You are already dead, but you will suffer more than death can ever give you. You will feel every tear, every heartache, every ounce of pain we suffered, and you will feel it for an eternity.'

Rick pushed Michael from behind as Rosie carved the knife

around his heart, slicing it into bleeding ribbons. There was minimal distance between the three connected bodies as Michael's eyes closed, bearing an intensity of strangled, stabbing excruciation. Michael was not dying. How can anyone die twice? This was a far greater adversity, ceaseless, wretched agony, unremitting hurt and the grievous deadweight of self-condemnation. Two innocent people who had been sent on a reluctant journey of self-destruction, caught up and tangled forever in the ruination of Michael's torrid imagination, were leaving him with the inescapable responsibility of regret.

CHAPTER FORTY

The Outcast

Every grain of every spadeful of soil was a weight bearing heavily on Michael's body. He was gradually being consumed by the gravity of his actions. Spade after spade was shovelled into his deep, open grave and the pressure was pulverising his entire spirit and soul. His drawn-out death journey was littered with pain and misfortune, atrocities that would not have manifested without his lurid existence. From every conceivable angle there were prods of tormenting fire searing his dying body, prods of misgiving and self-reproach.

'C'mon mate it's your turn, hurry up. We all want to have a go at the bitch!' The surly, tattooed man pushed Michael forward with brutish force and there in front of him, through the intoxicating mists of the underworld, was the source of the harrowing wails curdling his burning blood. Michael was once again faced with his ignoble legacy, another travesty which was manufactured through his simplistic wrongdoings. People he had never met during the course of his life fitted into his fragmented jigsaw past as the grave consequences of his misdeeds materialised.

Aisha Khusa was repeatedly raped by a fraudulent soothsayer and had given birth to a bastard child. Surine Devata had travelled the globe, only to heal Michael's possessed suffering. Michael's contrived stories had plagued his parents and legitimately paid for

Surine's divine influence to rid the country of evil spells and even solve the quandary of infertility, praying upon the vulnerabilities of entire communities that believed their dawn would never come as they lived under the darkness of the evils conjured by witchcraft and black magic.

Aisha's dark, saucer-shaped eyes bore the stressed burden of a contaminated and catastrophic life. Her nose was weeping blood upon the white sheets of her bed, crushed and jarred out of joint from burly fists that paid for the pleasure of female domination and substantiated their fragile masculinity. She was naked, her inflamed skin carpeted with festering lacerations, each one a war wound from the men who had conquered and blemished her fragile limbs. Brave men who fought on the battlefield of her body with all their might and fearless courage overcoming their shortcomings and leaving big, erect and victorious, having further destroyed a woman who had been outcast from her community into the begrimed world of prostitution.

Aisha opened her mouth, her teeth were cracked and chipped, resembling an eerie grey cemetery. No words came out. Her lips were burst and her tongue was too swollen from the forced intrusions of men paying for the pleasure of inflicting subjugated misery and filling her throat with whatever pleased them, but still her distressed voice entered Michael's head and tortured his sinking mind and spirit.

'You killed me, Michael. Your deeds lost me my family and I became an outcast, a piece of unwanted trash, vile and unworthy of love. You had me raped day after day after day. You brought Surine's evil into my life. It was you that raped me, you have to have the responsibility of what happened in my life. All those men queuing behind you will beat me, burn me and hurt me for an eternity and spit in my face as they leave. Every punch I suffer will quake your afterlife, all my bruises will puncture your body and all my bleeding wounds will drain your poisoned heart. You will violently suffer every indignity that you've put me through until the end of time. This is what you did. This is now your fate. Leave me now and begin the suffering you deserve.'

A stream of teary blood trickled from her battered eye as Michael drifted away from the devastating scene and the surly, muscled man behind him in the queue took his turn and shrouded her with his hulking frame, viciously crunching and fracturing the bone of her pelvis as he forced himself inside her. Aisha maintained eye contact with Michael. This was the haunted stare of another chapter as she convulsed underneath a hefty assailant demanding satisfaction. Another piece of the serpentine and tangled biography Michael had unknowingly initiated.

My Brief Affair

'Why are you doing this to me? Why are you making me suffer the pain of my past? I want to die, I'm already dying. Just let me go, let me die! Take this diseased life of mine and let me face my destiny. I can't see any more, I just want to die. Please let me die! Why are you torturing me like this? I made all the mistakes I was given the will to make. Lives have been marred, irretrievable paths created and destinies affected but never knowingly destroyed. I understand the ripples I created and I know I cannot retrieve them. If I could, I would go back and change it all. I'm sorry. I fall at your feet and I give you back the life you granted me. My brief affair in this world is over!'

There was stillness. It was a darker, bleaker place than death. Not a sound except the reverberation of thoughts and memories, echoes from the past all gathered in one place, all of them present and yet not apparent. Every touch, heartache, aggression and most insignificant emotion gathered in its entirety, floating in this black void of nothingness. A raven, silent, vacuous abyss with a sky adrift with feather light lanterns, glowing in the morbid darkness with faces, scenarios, entire episodes, words and expressions ensconced for an eternity within each one, vibrating through time and space, rippling their effect in a sea of circumstance. This was the personal memoir of a human life, winding down to its withering moments of creation, with the lifelong oscillation picturesquely drawn out in a million images, each one connected, related and a consequence of another.

As Michael viewed the scroll of his legacy with a reluctant fascination, an intense heat scorched the sombre environment and a single pained tear swelled in his eye. His surroundings were scorched, melted and set ablaze by a vindictive fire, intent on nothing less than obliteration. Rodin's reincarnated masterpiece bellowed with pride, his anguished lovers immortalised in time and now a magnificent reprise, once again ending in human destruction.

Somehow, through a celestially heightened mind on the brink of expiration, Michael knew the gasp charging from his seared and burst lungs was his final breath. There was no salute necessary, instead a mutual respect and solemn goodbye as it puffed from his charred mouth and silently evaporated into the relentless fire.

My brief affair with love and life,
Bravely anticipated and blindly stepped.
A blindfolded journey, with fate dragged days.
But always time to mend my ways.
Broken rules with determination and so many goodbyes
Anguish, drama and deceit decorated with lies.
Unmitigated laughter, courage, tears and strife.
This was my life.
Flirtations with adventure and passion, with so many question whys
And yet I discovered such Magic, Wonder & Surprise.
Tortured Mind and Tortured love, they paved the miles
Each and every day and not a day without smiles.
I screamed into existence and I cry into death.

Take everything I have as I give you my final breath.
Goodbye world, you taught me well now there is nothing left to dwell
This was my brief affair with love and life.
I bid you farewell.

The Angel

Blackness. No sound, no smell, nothing to touch, just sullen gloomy darkness. This was death. An eternity of wandering in the dark with no direction, no purpose and no belonging. A timeless Cimmerian shade flowing through veins that were once crimson red, shrouding the colours of imagination into pallid nothingness and banishing thoughts into a bleak abyss. Bereft of emotions with no apprehension of the present, past or future. It was an endless nightfall, with no hope of dawn. Suddenly and with a disrespect for death, a solitary glimmer severed the starless black velvet, abruptly slicing through the dimness and overwhelming Michael's eyes. A shine so distant, so out of reach and yet so brightly flickering a ray of promise.

Was this hope impetuously emanating a path or was this the chicanery of the afterlife, a mirage of the tomb, the trickery of death itself, mocking the damned?

'*Hope will guide you and hope will keep you alive. Deep, deep inside your heart you have to believe you will be OK again. Even if you only have one tiny ounce of hope left that one day you will heal, then you need to hang onto that because that one ounce of hope will get you through, that single ounce will give you a reason to live. Sometimes all you need is hope.*'

Familiar words punctuated the darkness with shards of light and kindled an obscure, long-forgotten memory from Michael's days of living. Maybe it was hours, days, months or centuries ago but the words were comforting, exhaling warmth and benevolence, almost a hand reaching out to death across oceans of time and bewilderment. Could this be Michael's Angel or was it a torturous, unredeemed flashback to a life once lived?

'Hope will guide you and hope will keep you alive. Deep, deep inside your heart you have to believe you will be OK again. Even if you only have one tiny ounce of hope left that one day you will heal, then you need to hang onto that because that one ounce of hope will get you through, that single ounce will give you a reason to live. Sometimes all you need is hope.'

The words were getting closer, piercing the doom with their calmness and sense of expectation. The shimmering glow needled through Michael's eyelids and he reluctantly opened his eyes. The darkness was fragmented, scattered as the shine conquered the land. Michael felt the welcome intimacy of a human hand wrapped around his.

'Hello Michael, I've been waiting for you. You're ok now, you're safe. Hope was in your heart. Sometimes all you need is hope'

Michael's voice grated, stinging his dry throat as he forced a whisper 'are you my angel, am I in heaven'

'No Michael, I'm a nurse and you're in hospital, you've been unconscious for weeks, you were in a terrible fire. Somehow, I knew you would come back, I knew you would survive, hope has kept you alive'

The glistening shine was coming from the nurse's silver badge as it wavered in front of Michael's squinting sensitive eyes, reflecting the bright lights from the ceiling. As she moved forward to adjust his pillow, he took a peek at her badge: it said 'Dawn McCracken'.

'Thank you Dawn, you are my angel' said Michael.

Epilogue

The universe is an infinite buzzing lake of continuance, perturbed by every minuscule happening catapulted into it. From the most insignificant spoken word to the greatest earth-shattering skirmishes, there are ripples created that will remodel billions of particles, composing alternative symphonies that themselves will echo through the undefined corridors of time and space.

The entirety of the cosmos is being remodelled every millionth of a second, and will change with everything from an effortless playground taunt to the extremities of world devastation and calamity. Every breath you take bears a significance within your own world and the whole world itself.

You are literally breathing life into the Universe, rippling changes through time and leaving an indelible mark that will forever remain your personal legacy, yet you will live and die never knowing you initiated it.